Jakarta
Missing

❖ ❖

BY JANE KURTZ

❖ ❖

Greenwillow Books

An Imprint of HarperCollins*Publishers*

Jakarta Missing

Copyright © 2001 by Jane Kurtz
For information address HarperCollins Children's Books,
a division of HarperCollins Publishers, 1350 Avenue of the Americas,
New York, NY 10019.
www.harpercollins.com
The text of this book is set in Garamond 3.

Library of Congress Cataloging-in-Publication Data
Kurtz, Jane.
Jakarta missing / by Jane Kurtz.
p.   cm.
"Greenwillow Books."
Summary: When her sister, star-athlete Jakarta, finally joins them, Dakar feels
much safer and happier in Cottonwood, North Dakota, where she and their
parents are living for a year, but she still longs for their home in Africa.
ISBN 0-06-029401-9 (trade). ISBN 0-06-029402-7 (lib. bdg.)
[1. Sisters—Fiction.   2. Family life—North Dakota—Fiction.
3. Homesickness—Fiction.   4. Courage—Fiction.   5. Women athletes—
Fiction.   6. Moving, Household—Fiction.   7. North Dakota—Fiction.
8. Schools—Fiction.]   I. Title.
PZ7.K9626 Jak 2001   [Fic]—dc21   00-056195

1   2   3   4   5   6   7   8   9   10   First Edition ✗

To Jonathan, who took
60,000 basketball shots one summer
and thus became my #1 basketball hero

PROLOGUE

FROM DAKAR'S BOOK
OF LISTS AND THOUGHTS

Spring

Okay. Dad was right. Anyone *would* have to be crazy to want to live through this kind of winter. I know now about days when the hair inside your nose freezes and you feel like someone stuck a toothbrush up there. I know about days when the wind hits you in the face so hard that you gasp for breath and think you must still be asleep and dreaming of Antarctica. The snow squeaks like Styrofoam when you walk to school, and you can see the breath of every car that passes.

"I knew you'd be sorry," I can hear him saying. But I'm not sorry.

Winter made me feel *solid*. Before, I was always a ghost, slipping through places, never leaving a mark. I didn't belong any of those places. And they closed up behind me like water.

Besides, if I hadn't lived through torturous winter, would spring make my eyes sting with joy?

❖ *I* ❖

Outside the back door there's a vanilla puff of a tree right beside a coral one, like two ice-cream cones. The trees remind me of my leaf quest, which did and did not work.

Is North Dakota as pretty as Kenya can be when the rains finally come and wash the red dust off the flowers? No. But getting through winter makes everything seem glorious. Yesterday the ash trees laid down a green carpet that I could dance on, and I didn't even care when Mom said it was because of a fungus, since this spring was so wet.

No, I'm not sorry. But I am embarrassed to admit that I still haven't stopped turning that one moment in the gym over and over in my mind— like the end of a movie . . . but a movie where I get to be the director, so it always ends the way I decide.

Jakarta dribbles wildly down the court. Sometimes she takes it right to the basket, charging straight at her defender until the last minute, when she steps to the left and goes up, up, flicking the basketball toward the basket with her left hand. The ball slides in and catches on nothing but the bottom of the net. I hear its whispering swish, just before the gym fills with a giant roaring. Other times Jakarta pulls up at the three-point line and launches the ball into the air. It soars in a high arc, up and in. Always, always in.

❖ ❖

ONE

❖ ❖

Dakar stood at the top of the stairs and held her breath. No voices. No music. No rustling pages. She wanted . . . the click of a fingernail clipper. The tiniest creak of a chair sending little splinters into the silence. No. Nothing.

She clutched her throat melodramatically. Deadly cholera had swept through the house while she was asleep. She was the only survivor. Nothing to do but go down . . . into the valley of dry bones.

"Stop it, Dakar," she told herself. "You're scaring me." She grabbed on to the railing. Was this what books called a banister? She'd always wondered, reading those books, what it would be like to slide down a banister. In her imagination it had been a little like flying. Now, staring down at the polished wood, she felt stupid with fear.

"It is a poor life in which there is no fear." Dad had that pinned on a scrap of paper above his desk. And he said it to her one time—the afternoon the elephant charged them. Dad also thought that if you gave in, even once, to things like fear and

❖ 3 ❖

injustice and cruelty, they would get a toehold and come back the next time double strong.

All right. A banister couldn't possibly be as scary as an elephant. Dakar closed her eyes and scooted herself onto the railing. But what if she slid off halfway down and split her lip? What if she went off the end so hard she sprained her ankle? She hastily scooted back off. "You're such a worrywart," her big sister, Jakarta, would say. "Dakar, the worrymeister." By some kind of magic, Jakarta seemed to have inherited 100 percent of Dad's risk genes.

Thinking about Jakarta made Dakar seasick with longing so that she had to sit down on the top step and put her hands on either side to steady herself, still surprised to feel carpet there. "Isn't this luxurious?" Mom had said the first day they walked into the house. "We've never had carpet before." She'd stretched out flat in the middle of the living room, laughing as she tickled her palms with carpet strands. But Dakar missed the cool, dark floors of the Nairobi house. She missed the geckos like ghost tongues flicking and licking up the walls. She wasn't even sure she knew how to make friends with a two-story house. More than anything else, of course, she missed Jakarta.

How *could* Jakarta have decided to stay in

Kenya? Maybe . . . Dakar chewed her fingernail thoughtfully, sadly . . . was Jakarta sick of always having to take care of a worrymeister little sister? She glanced up at the banister. Okay. She'd do it. She could become less of a wart, she just knew it.

"Dakar, you think too much," Jakarta always said.

"Don't think, don't think," Dakar told herself as she climbed onto the banister again. She didn't dare look down.

She let go. Her stomach whooshed up so far she could taste it, and then she flew off the end, staggered a few steps, and stumbled forward. She landed right in front of the dining room table. Mom, who always sat at the table and read in the mornings, was not there.

Dakar stood up and rubbed her knees. She knew they'd grow big black-and-blue bruises, and she felt a slight tingling of pride. She'd done it—for Jakarta.

Where was Mom? She felt a tingling of nervousness. "Dakar's famous overactive imagination is at it again," Jakarta would say. But it really was a mysterious morning, wasn't it? She cautiously moved to the back door. Her father was chopping wood. His arms rose and fell, and for a second Dakar thought of women pounding corn. He was singing a mournful Celtic tune, not one of the sea chanties or West African songs he used to sing all the time.

Dakar watched him warily. Hadn't Dad sung this very song when he was making waffles on the morning he told them they were going to leave Kenya? "We've decided it might be time to spend a year or two on the border of North Dakota and Minnesota," he'd said, reaching for Mom's hand over the mango syrup. "We'll be living only one long day's drive from where your mother grew up. Hey, we've explored the world . . . now let's explore the land of ten thousand lakes and the land of the flickertail."

Jakarta had instantly said, "No. I'm not going." She had at least fifteen reasons, she said, starting with not being able to make friends in the U.S. Jakarta had said the letters very distinctly. "Youuu. Essss."

Dakar had wanted to say, "I won't go, either," but she desperately wanted the four of them together, and she was pretty sure Jakarta would change her mind. So, instead, she'd said, "But what will you *do*?"

"I'll write articles about all my African research," Dad said cheerfully. "Something I've been putting off for years. We've picked a town not far from both the University of North Dakota and a branch of the University of Minnesota, so I'll have resources." He laughed his rumbling laugh. "It also has an airport thirty minutes away in case I need to get out of town fast."

Dakar sighed. But Jakarta hadn't changed her mind. So here she was, and the whole family wasn't together, anyway, because here Jakarta *wasn't*.

Suddenly Dad looked up, stopped right in the middle of a mournful line, and waved. Then he bent, scooped up an armful of wood, and walked toward her, smiling. She had always thought that his smile was bedazzling sunlight and that if she could only get close enough to it, she could get warm and never worry, worry, worry about things again. When he got inside the door, she ran to him and put both her arms around one of his, leaning her head against his shoulder. His beard smelled of incense, and his shoulder smelled of soap and sweat. "Getting some breakfast?" he asked, holding her back so he could look down into her face.

She glanced into his eyes. What was that look? She didn't like it, didn't like it at all. "No." She hadn't known she was going to say it until the word came out. "I have to get to school early to work on a project that Melanie and I are doing together. It's . . . um . . . about different knots. Sailor knots, I mean. The sea, you know." The sea? Where did that come from? Dakar, you amaze me, she thought.

He didn't try to stop her. She waited for him to say, "Wait! You have to eat breakfast," as she crammed her books into the bag, but he didn't say anything. Then suddenly he was kneeling beside her, putting his hand over hers. "Dakar," he said.

"No," she wanted to say. "No. Don't say it. Whatever it is." She pulled her hand out from under his. She wanted to put her hands over her ears.

"There's been a bombing," he said. "We tried most of the night to get in touch with someone at the school. But you know how phone lines can be over there even when things are at their very technological best. Don't worry about Jakarta." In spite of his words, there was a trapped sound at the back of his voice, and Dakar had a quick thought of a moth in a cage. "Really," he said, "there's no need to worry yet. You know how the phone lines can be."

How phone lines can be in Ah-free-kah? She drew the word out in her mind, the way people would say it there. Why hadn't Mom come into her room to rock her for a minute and whisper that everything was going to be fine? "I gotta go," she said.

She was out the door, running down the smooth sidewalk of this square block. When Dad had said they were going back to the States, Dakar had instantly imagined herself as Georgia O'Keeffe, striding along the desert under an azure sky. Or maybe living in a city where skyscrapers stood so close together you could stretch out your arms and touch buildings with both hands . . . or somewhere that smelled of sea and fog, in an old house creaky with ghosts. She had not imagined Cottonwood, North Dakota, at all. But here she was.

She opened her mouth and let air whoosh inside it. What was happening to Jakarta right this minute? Don't think. Don't think. Without thinking, she scooped up a handful of gravel and flung it at Melanie's window, where it clattered and pinged.

"Kid-hey!" She could see Melanie's pale face at the window, knew from the shape of her mouth the word she had said. A moment later the door opened. "Get in here." Melanie pulled Dakar inside, laughing. "What are you doing? What happened to your knees?"

Dakar crossed her eyes and made a fish mouth. "Didn't you always want to try that thing with the window? They do it in books, you know, whenever someone wants to rouse somebody."

"I've never known anyone who read so much. Anyhow, why are you early?" Melanie tugged on her hand. "Whatever. I wanted you to look at this catalog, anyway. I am in total love with these clothes. Did you eat?"

Dakar nodded yes, but Melanie wasn't looking at her. Melanie would wear all red to school, if she felt like it, and not care if people made fire siren sounds as she walked down the hall. Melanie said just what she was thinking. The first thing she had ever said to Dakar was "Why aren't you black?"

"Why should I be?"

"You grew up in Africa. And your name. I expected you to be black."

"Well, I'm not."

"Yeah, I see that. Wanna come to my house and get something to drink?"

Jakarta wouldn't have said yes. But Dakar had said yes to Melanie, yes to pop and Kool-Aid instead of powdered milk and Stoney Tangawizi. "Adorned with three tiny rosettes," Melanie was saying, now. "Isn't that cool? Breeze tissue linen. I want this blouse. What do you think?"

The woman wearing the blouse had bare feet.

She didn't look like the type to get worms in her feet, or thorns. Her face was serene. "Expensive," Dakar said, wishing people could order feet from catalogs. Or faces. Serene faces.

Melanie wrinkled up her face. "At least you didn't say 'for cute.' But I didn't expect you to be practical. Everyone around here is so extremely boringly practical. Here, close your eyes. I want you to hear these colors."

Dakar closed her eyes.

"Not just white and black and red," Melanie said. "Cinnabar. Dusty plum. Oooo, cypress. What color is that?"

"Mmm." Dakar felt as if she were floating. Dusty plum. The dust was swirling, turning the sky to grainy gray. Where was she? Camels swaying through the dust with melancholy eyes.

"Olive," Melanie said. "Coral, ivory, flax, chamois. Shhhhhham-waw." She rolled the word over her tongue and lips.

Coral- and plum-colored blossoms cascading over a wall . . . what did that remind her of? Somewhere she'd been with Jakarta. "I'm so sorry, my sweet one. So sorry." Dakar's eyes flew open. Jakarta had just spoken to her. What would Jakarta be doing speaking to her, unless, unless . . .

Dakar scrambled to her feet, almost knocking the chair over.

"What's wrong?" Melanie leaped up, too.

"Let's go."

On the way to school she felt herself shivering. "What would you do if something scared you?" she asked. "I mean, really scared you."

Melanie knew how to make her eyes go so wide open that she reminded Dakar of a cartoon person. "Around here," she said, "hardly anything *really* scary ever happens. If it did, I guess someone would give a speech about our brave pioneer ancestors or how community spirit would help us pull through."

Dakar laughed. This place did seem safe—nothing like walking down a sidewalk in downtown Nairobbery, where she didn't dare wear any jewelry because one of her teachers had gotten his arm stabbed through by someone trying to get his watch.

"But," Melanie said, "if I was really and truly scared, I'd go right to my mom." She stared at Dakar with wide-open green eyes. Light green, Dakar thought. Shadow green. Shiny green. Beetle green. Cinnabar green. Nah, cinnabar probably wasn't even green.

Dakar wrapped her arms around her shoulders. How could she just go to school, not knowing if Jakarta was safe or not? Maybe it wasn't a coincidence that the idea of sliding down the banister had popped into her mind before she even knew about the bombing. Was she supposed to be getting the message that there was something she could be doing besides worrying? "Don't mope, do something," Dad always said. "Big problems require big solutions. You are the hero of your own life." Too bad his younger daughter was heroic as snail slime.

Heroic as snail slime? But wait a minute! Wasn't it the simpleton, the weak youngest kid in the family who usually turned out to be the hero in the old stories? For a second she couldn't breathe. After all this time was the universe trying to send her on another *quest*?

She put her hands cautiously on her head. On the other hand, maybe deadly cholera had dried up her brains. No, wait. Think this through. People like Odysseus and Gilgamesh knew exactly what they wanted from their quests—they knew they were heroes from the start. But what about Moses standing in front of the burning bush saying, "Send my brother, 'cause I don't know how to say things right"? What about Isaiah saying, "Woe is me, for I am a man of unclean lips?"

There were heroes who felt puny when the story started. And who didn't know what to do. They just . . . started. "Here I am," Isaiah said. "Send me." Okay, Dakar thought as they reached the middle school steps. Send me.

Nothing happened. She had absolutely zero inspiration about what to do next.

Okay. What if she was supposed to do, say, three really brave things? She was pretty sure that had worked once. If it worked this time, maybe Jakarta would not only be safe but also come home and all four of them would be together again, which is what Dakar wanted more than anything in the world. Okay. She knew just the place for starting a quest. "Hey, I'm going in the high school door," she said.

Melanie looked startled and a little scared. "We're not supposed to."

"I know." The two words sounded so bold that Dakar flushed.

"Wow," Melanie said thoughtfully. "Well, maybe if they catch us, they won't do anything. They'll just think you came from Africa and you didn't know better . . . and we'll say I tried to stop you, but it all happened too fast." She giggled.

Dakar put her hands to her cheeks as she turned the corner and walked toward the corner of the building. Her face was so hot it was probably purple. What if they got marched to the principal's office? What if he was a growling, scowling gorilla of a man? What if he yelled at them and handed them instant detention? What if someone called her parents? Weird—Dakar, the Good Kid, breaking the rules. Dakar, the Follower, striding along with Melanie pattering after her.

She wished she *felt* bold. Bold enough to ask Melanie the questions that were bouncing around her brain. But what if your mom was scared of the same thing? What if it was a real thing like a bomb, something people should be scared of? What if you'd gotten out of practice talking to your mom because you knew what it was like to go without her for months and months? What if you'd learned a long time ago, not because anyone told you but because you somehow knew knew knew, that some things you shouldn't talk about because they would just make everybody too sad?

✤ ✤

TWO

✤ ✤

As they walked around the corner, Dakar grabbed Melanie's arm. There was no way they looked as cool as these high school students. They should be planning exactly what they wanted to say when they were stopped. She winced, but her feet just kept going, and somehow they were walking up the stairs and through the door. To Dakar's astonishment, even with a beefy high school teacher standing right there, no one even seemed to look at them. She wanted to laugh. After that hairy speech on the first day of school, it was no big deal to use the high school door.

Foo. That was almost too easy. Or . . . was it *charmed*? She knew where she needed to go next, straight over to the wall—the wall o' jocks, as Jakarta would call it. "We saw this on the orientation tour," Melanie said. "How come you wanted to see it again?"

Dakar stared with awe at the names and numbers. Every person up there was like a modern-day Odysseus or Gilgamesh—all those athletes pitting

✤ 16 ✤

themselves against obstacles and only sometimes getting a tiny bit of glory, while everyone else sat around and tossed olive pits at them. Sometimes you needed to be around people like that to soak up their courage and confidence.

She suddenly knew what else had struck her the first time she saw this wall. At all her schools it bothered her that every year there were new athletes, new teams just, well, sweeping away all the old heroes and all those soaring memories. It bugged her the way someone could be so great and then disappear without a ripple.

But once your name was on this wall, you were solid. You were forever. Lois Yellowbird had the record for the fifty-yard dash. She wouldn't stop for any golden apples thrown on the path by her enemies to distract her. No, she must have streaked across the line, hair flying. Zoe Thureen and Natalie Thureen each had a relay record. Were they sisters? Cousins? Was quickness in family genes?

Dakar took a few steps and looked at the middle section. The boys' basketball team had won state championships in 1947 and 1974. Interesting pattern. Just coincidence? The bodies of the boys on the winning teams were drawn in basketball poses. Photos of their heads were pasted on. Girls' basketball had no state championships, but Promise Johnson held the record for most points in a regular season.

"What's so great about a *wall*?" Melanie persisted. "I'm sure you saw stuff a thousand times more interesting than this in Africa."

It was true. She had seen incredible things. Melanie didn't need to know that at least half the things had scared her.

"Notice, the Cottonwood Wildcats' best sport is hockey," Melanie said, waving at the next section. "And it is not an accident that *hockey* rhymes with *cocky*. But my cousins say the hockey team is no way even going to regionals this year. They say, even so, everyone can't wait for hockey season because the football team is sooo lousy. I told them *I* can wait."

No soccer, Dakar noticed. What would Jakarta do even if Dakar pulled off a quest that *did* manage to get her here? Yikes. Speaking of the quest, no ideas were coming to her. "Come on," she said, deflated. "We're going to be late for class."

As she got close to the middle school hall, she began to ease one foot in front of the other. She was a tracker in the bushland. One false step, and the elephant's ears would fan out. She imagined she could hear the muffled snort of a lion, breathing threats and slaughter. Instead, a locker slammed. She stopped, listening to the voices.

"That's your new hair thingie, right? For cute!"

"Quit that—you almost made me drop my books. Why do you always have to be body-checking everyone?"

"Borrow me a quarter, hey?"

Dakar glanced at Melanie, and they laughed. Then she felt a splash of guilt whitewashing her heart. Jakarta had been her rock, her hiding place, and she not only had let herself be torn away from Jakarta, but was making a friend.

She tried to remember when she'd ever had a friend like Melanie. In her first school, which happened to be a boarding school in Ethiopia, all she ever wanted to do was tag along after Jakarta—Jakarta, the queen. Jakarta, the one who thought up all the games and assigned all the parts. When Dakar had to spend time with her roommates, she made herself small and unsquirmy. If Jakarta ever got impatient with having a little sister bumping along behind her, Dakar went off and pretended to be a horse, galloping through the grass that swished and grabbed at her legs. In the international schools in Egypt and Kenya, she was the type of kid who skittered at the backs of classes and never said anything out loud on purpose. Just a quiet kid hanging on the edge.

With Melanie, everything was different. The first day of school, right after homeroom, kids had bunched around Dakar's locker, cornering her. Of course, it didn't take much to make her feel cornered, a water buffalo staring into golden lion eyes, knowing by instinct that she must not run. She heard them asking questions, but she was so nervous that their voices just sounded like babbling *waah-waah-waah* until one boy's voice pushed over the rest. "Hey, do you speak some weird language?"

At first she thought she wouldn't bother to answer. But he was leaning against her locker, and she wasn't going to be able to get her books out until he moved, so she said, "Yeah, I'm a polyglot. *Wakati umeketi, funga mkanda.*"

Babble, babble, *waah-waah-waah* . . . "What did she say? What did she say? Say it again. What does it mean?"

Suddenly Melanie was there, flying through the crowd like an avenging angel, shoving people, hollering, "You guys are being so stupid." She gave the boy leaning against the locker a push. "You— you speak weird languages all the time."

"Me?" He scowled at her. "I'm not even taking Spanish."

Melanie slammed her own locker open, shut and whirled around. "No!" Her voice could wither flowers. "Anything but Spanish. But you say things like 'Borrow me a quarter, hey?' What kind of language is that?"

Everyone had laughed, and their laughter made Dakar feel strong. "It means," she said, "it means . . . in the jungle, the mighty lion weeps." She had walked away grandly, listening to the sudden silence behind her.

"Fierce!" Melanie said, running to catch up. "Who taught you how to say that?"

Dakar just shrugged. The truth was that the words were printed on the back of the Kenya Airways seat in front of her, and she had whispered, "*Wakati umeketi, funga mkanda,*" over and over to herself when she got bored with sitting cramped in the airplane seat for eight hours. The English words were underneath: "Fasten seat belt while seated."

"We better hurry," Melanie said now. "See you in math."

Dakar nodded. The halls had gotten crowded.

She pulled her invisible cloak around her so no one would purposely bounce into her and knock her books out of her arms, hurried up the stairs, and slipped into English class, about a minute late. She could feel herself blushing as she sneaked to her seat. "We'll be going over outlines today," Ms. Olson was saying. "For your first reports." Dakar grimaced. How could she care about outlines when Jakarta was in danger? She eased her lists and thoughts book out of her backpack and made her own outline as Ms. Olson talked.

What I miss most
1. Kenya
    a. Trees—the one Jakarta and I called a frangi-pangi tree with its creamy yellow and white flowers . . . and the strange way the lavender flowers come out on the jacaranda trees.
    b. The red roofs of houses. Red puddles. Red clay on the rug.
    c. The sounds of the Kikuyu village when I woke up—birds and roosters and lambs and people calling to each other.
    d. The ginger taste of Stoney Tangawizi peppering my mouth. Why doesn't Coca-Cola sell Stoney Tangawizi in America?

She doodled for a moment and then kept writing.

2. Ethiopia
    a. The little pods of the eucalyptus trees that Jakarta and I used for teacups.
    b. Thick fog in the gray-green mountains.
    c. The cozy, safe attic where Jakarta and I played paper dolls.
3. Egypt
    a. Sneaking navel oranges out of the dining hall to eat after Jakarta's soccer practice.

Dakar closed her eyes as the smell of sweat and oranges washed over her. The oranges were brilliantly colored and so full of juice you choked as you bit down on each piece. Then she started writing again.

    b. Can't remember anything else at the moment, but Ms. Olson just said if you have an "a" you have to have a "b."
4. Jakarta.
5. Jakarta.
6. Jakarta.

She sighed. Had she really heard Jakarta's voice speaking to her back at Melanie's house? And could quests really change the course of the universe? Mrs. Yoder, the girls' dorm mother at boarding school, might say this was heathen thinking, but even Mrs. Yoder talked about how everything you did—or even *thought*—mattered. And how mysterious the whole universe really was.

". . . finish up tomorrow," Ms. Olson was saying. "Don't forget to be thinking about a topic for your report." Dakar slid her book back in her backpack and stood up. The wall hadn't given her any inspiration about what to do next. What she really needed was one of those wizened old Baba Yaga types who unexpectedly show up and give instructions to the hero.

Baba Yaga! Of course. She almost laughed. She swerved in the opposite direction from her second-period class and hurried down the hall, imagining herself as a princess, sweeping the corridor with her silver-and-red cloak. Lucky thing she'd been given the gift of invisibility at birth.

Quickly now. Down two sets of stairs. She was running by the time she got to the place where soap and taco meat and sour washcloth smells were strong and where she could hear the *shhhick, shiiick* of a knife being rubbed against something. She stopped, panting, put her backpack on the counter, and looked into the kitchen, her elbows on her book. "Hey," she said, softly.

"Mercy." The cook's voice was loud and had a kind of roll to it, but she didn't look up from her knives. "Lord have mercy on all your children, and especially on those who have to put up with the pestilence that stalks in darkness, the destruction that wastes at noonday, and students who creep around buildings on quiet feet."

"Don't you remember me?" Dakar asked.

"Should I remember? Should I remember?" The cook began chopping onions, rocking the knife back and forth.

Dakar leaned into the familiar smell. "I'm the one who liked your chili last week when everyone complained it was too hot. I showed you my ring from Ethiopia. You said you'd never forget me."

"Ah." The cook chopped deftly, the way women in Ethiopia and Kenya knew how to chop onions. "Ah, yes. The Africa child. Don't you hear that bell ringing? Grab hold of your education, I tell you. Grab hold and hang on, and don't ever let anything shake you off. Go on, now. You can still make it."

"I have to ask you something first." Dakar felt her breath coming quickly, the way it did when she was a centaur, feeling the grass against her leg muscles as she ran, somehow both horse and human at the same time.

"Ask then." The cook muttered something that Dakar couldn't hear. "Ask, ask."

Dakar tried to pull that moment at Melanie's table back into focus. "If you heard someone's voice. Heard it very distinctly, I mean. Someone that isn't even in the same country as you. Do you think it's true that . . ." A fly was buzzing in the kitchen somewhere. She'd hardly seen any flies here. How had one managed to get inside and also stay hidden from the cook and her sharp knives?

Melanie was scared of the cook because of those knives. But the knives made Dakar remember the teenage boys who worked in the Maji kitchen to make money for school. They would wave the kitchen knives at her and say, "We'll cut off your ears." They laughed if she shrieked or squealed, as she quickly learned not to do. Of course, they would never really and truly hurt her, but they did use the knives to cut the heads off chickens. Dakar shuddered. Not the time to think of that—the chickens squawking and flapping their blood around the yard.

"Africa child? Are you gone to class?"

Dakar wrapped her arms around her backpack and hugged it. "Okay, it's this. My mom says that when her mother died, she heard her mother speak to her plainly. You know. After it turned out her mother was already dead. Maybe my grandma's spirit was still hovering for a few hours, or something. Well, I know it can happen because it happened to my mom, but do you think that's the only time you would hear a person's voice so clearly? If the person was dead?"

The cook began to hum. Dakar listened. After a few minutes she thought she would have to just go to class after all. But then the woman pointed the long knife at Dakar and said, "The earth and the firmament are full of the glory of God, I do know. I also know glory has such mysterious ways. Such mysterious ways. You never know where a bit of glory is going to pop up or why. I do know that."

" 'The heavens are telling the glory of God,' " Dakar said. " 'And the firmament proclaims his handiwork. Day to day pours forth speech, and night to night declares knowledge.' Psalms nineteen, one and two. I learned it in school in Ethiopia."

The cook chuckled. "You must have gone to some school there. Life's a miry bog, Africa child.

A dry and weary land. You're going to need knowledge to get through this life. Go to class."

Dakar put her book on her head and balanced it there. "A lot of Ethiopians get insulted if you call them African," she said. "I don't know why, but they do. I was actually born in West Africa, though, where the sand was soft and fine as flour and where the rooms of our house were sometimes so steamy and hot that my father's glasses would slide from his nose in a river of sweat. That's what my mother says, anyway. And I just now lived in Kenya. So you can call me Africa child." She turned, her books still on her head, and moved off with those gliding steps she and Jakarta used to practice. Jakarta! She jerked her head, and the book tumbled off.

THREE

Half an hour before lunch Dakar decided she might have to lie down in the middle of the classroom and perish from hunger. But it was good to think about the gnawing in her stomach, something powerful enough to take her mind from the worry, worry, worry.

When she made it until the fourth-period bell without perishing after all, there was the cafeteria to think about. Melanie had lunch second half, so Dakar didn't have anyone to eat with. She always navigated the cafeteria carefully, "with absolute stealth," she whispered to herself. If she was lucky, she could get through lunch without having her tray bump any of the wild animals ("wildebeests," Jakarta would call them). She could find a place to sit where she wouldn't be noticed, never downwind where her fear could be scented.

She thought the afternoon classes would be the worst, but in fact she discovered that she was able to concentrate fiercely, not wanting—even though she did want—to hear Jakarta's voice again.

"Jagged," she whispered to herself as she walked down the hall after her last class. "I'm feeling jagged, jagged, jagged." She said the word *jagged* so many times in her mind that it began to sound like mush and not even like a word. And then she suddenly didn't feel jagged at all, but more like frozen. That was it—her stomach was frozen. Soon her heart would be, too. How long did it take ice to creep from stomach to heart, and what, exactly, would happen when her heart iced over?

"Dakar!" It was Melanie. "Hang on. Hey, what *did* happen to your knees?"

Dakar blushed. "Um . . . nothing."

"Want to go to my house?"

She could go home. They might have news. But they might not, and what would that be like? Like an elephant stepping on her heart.

"What's wrong?" Melanie said when they were walking. "In math class you were staring at Mr. Johnson as if he was a squid. A dead squid. Was someone evil to you at lunch?"

"It's Jakarta." Dakar said the words quickly so she wouldn't think about them first. "I think she's in trouble. I wish more than anything that she hadn't stayed in Kenya. Have I told you much about Jakarta?" She knew she hadn't. She felt guilty every time she even *thought* about telling Melanie any stories about Jakarta.

"Jakarta, your sister?" Melanie chewed her thumbnail. "Wow. What kind of trouble? What are you going to do?"

"Maybe we need to light a candle for her," Dakar said. "As the smoke drifts up and away, we'll send our thoughts for Jakarta up with the smoke." The idea of being able to communicate with Jakarta in some way made the frozen spots that had somehow leaped to her lungs a little easier to breathe around.

Making conversation with Melanie's mom was going to be tough. She'd only met her once before. Besides, Dakar was never good at knowing what to say to strangers, and it would be even harder now that she was feeling so jagged and jangly. She concentrated on pretending that she had a governess, that the governess was sweeping them through the kitchen, managing her. "Time for your supremely gracious smile now," the governess was saying to her. No, *chiding* her. *Chiding* was a great word. She gave Melanie's mom what she hoped was a gracious smile and patted Gingerpuff, who leaped up on the counter and wound herself into Dakar's fingers while Melanie pulled out some crackers and slathered cream cheese on them and then slipped a candle from a drawer marked "Emergencies."

"Okay," Melanie said as soon as they were settled on her bed. "We won't even eat our crackers yet. Tell me all about Jakarta." She struck a match and reached over with a flourish to light the candle. "I'll concentrate on sending my thoughts off," she added, closing her eyes.

Dakar settled back against Melanie's pink pillows. What had Malika said that time when Malika and Jakarta had done a candle ceremony and let Dakar sit in? The universe is flowing goodness all around you. Open to the universe. "Well," she started, "Jakarta was always there. By the time I was born, she was already four years old."

"How come they named her Jakarta?"

"My mom and dad adopted her when they were living in Indonesia. Anyway, Jakarta always took care of me. At boarding school. And in Maji, when the Allalonestone—" She stopped. This was bad. The Allalonestone was something between Dakar and Jakarta. Now Melanie was staring at her with those wide, amazed eyes, waiting to her to go on. But she couldn't talk about something so personal. "Uh . . ." she said, "it's a long story that has to do with my mom. I don't think we should think about my mom, because the candle smoke is for Jakarta."

She closed her eyes and tried to think. She and Jakarta had done everything together. Every move, every country that had to be left behind, every time when Dad went off on one of his adventures and she wondered if this was the time he wouldn't come home, Jakata was there. "I always felt so *safe* when Jakarta was in the bunk bed right above me," she whispered. "When I was scared of the way the wind whooshed in the trees outside, she'd lean over the edge and sing 'Barbry Allen' to me." Dakar hummed a few notes, then sang. " 'They climbed and climbed to the steeple top, 'til they could climb no higher. And then they twined in a true lovers' knot . . . ' " She realized she was waiting for Melanie to finish it off the way Jakarta would have, but of course Melanie didn't know the song.

"I wish you would quit *stopping* when you get to the good parts," Melanie said.

"Sorry," Dakar said. "Have you ever had anyone applaud for you? Not just a polite smattering of applause but really, really clapping?"

"Not yet."

"Me, either. But sometimes—" She stopped, embarrassed, forced herself to go on. "Sometimes I have dreams where thousands of people are clapping and yelling and whistling. Jakarta could make me feel that way. She and I would make up stories together all the time, and then one day, when I told her a story for the first time, she said 'You are great!' It made me feel . . . all *huge* inside."

"I like to dream that I'm having secret adventures," Melanie said. "I wish I could have one in real life."

"Mom says Jakarta read to me for four hours straight when we moved to Ethiopia, but I don't remember because I was too young. I do remember Maji, though. That's in Ethiopia. We moved there because of a cholera epidemic Dad wanted to study, and we stayed for a long time."

Melanie was a good listener. Maybe the quest was to make a true friend, Dakar thought. That was something hard and a bit scary. Having a true friend might keep the ice from getting to her heart. But to have a true friend, didn't you have to be willing to tell some secrets? Okay. She would tell Melanie three real things about Maji. Maybe how on rainy days she and Jakarta would climb into the attic and make up stories for the paper families they cut from Sears catalogs? The families lived in spider webs—American dads and moms and well-dressed little kids all in their charming catalog poses. Sitting by the wood stove, she and Jakarta would turn the pages of the catalog, picking the people they wanted and cutting them out. Then they would carry the people up the ladder into the attic. She and Jakarta had to be careful not to step off the rafters up there because their feet could go through the mud ceiling.

No, she'd rather tell about outside, about how the first thing they always did was check the passion fruit vines to see if any of the fruit was ripe. "If it was," she told Melanie, "we'd suck the sweetness and seeds out. The second thing was to check the false banana trees for little frogs that hid down where the rainwater collected. Once Jakarta had the idea that we should toilet-train the frogs so they could be better pets."

Melanie giggled. Dakar thought about the frogs, their cool skin against her palms. She and Jakarta usually had to hide the frogs. Any Ethiopians who saw the frogs would slap at the children's hands until they let the frogs go, would scold them in Amharic, and pull back in fear or disgust as the frogs scrambled away.

"The best thing about Maji," Dakar said, "was the water babies." They played water babies whenever they followed Dad down to the waterfall. The game started where the bushes by the path were thick and you had to be careful not to let stinging nettle touch your legs. The water babies grew curled up at the tops of ferns. She and Jakarta would pick them carefully and hold them, resting in their palms, until they got down to the river. While Dad talked to people at the mill, they'd make boats out of sticks. Dakar could still see the water whirling the boats away, she and Jakarta running after them, down the river, past the mill where people's grain got ground into flour. She could remember the fine, thin smell of the flour.

If the boats got stuck, they had to wade in and get them free. The cold water shocked the skin of her bare feet, hurting all the way to the tip of her tongue, but Jakarta said they had to save the water babies. She sighed.

"Don't stop," Melanie said.

So Dakar explained the game. "We would follow the water babies as far as we could. But finally we'd get to a place where the bushes were too thick and we couldn't follow. 'Say good-bye now,' Jakarta would say, and we would call, 'Good-bye. Good-bye.' I always asked her where they went, but she would say, 'It's a secret. I'll tell you someday.' "

Suddenly Dakar realized she was about to cry. She put the tip of her thumb in her mouth and bit it hard. That usually worked.

"Are you sending Jakarta your good thoughts?" Melanie whispered. "One of my aunts says, 'Trust the universe.'"

Dakar thought about that. Was it the same as when Mrs. Yoder said, "God loves you"? She had always tried to believe that God loved her, but sometimes it didn't seem possible. Probably Melanie's aunt had never seen some of the terrible things she'd seen—the man with his milky-white blind eyes reaching out as she went past, or the kids without arms or legs, begging on the sidewalks of the city. But Mrs. Yoder had seen those things, and she still believed that God loved people.

"Is this the first time you've been away from Jakarta?" Melanie asked.

"Except the first year Jakarta went to boarding school." As Dakar said the words, she suddenly thought about her one other true friend—a friend who, like Melanie, had looked at her with admiring eyes and let her make up almost all the games.

Gingerpuff scratched at the door, and Melanie got up, saying, "Little Miss Can't Decide if She Wants In or Out."

Her friend's name was Wondemu, and they played together all the time that year. But she had missed Jakarta too much. So she'd left Maji and followed Jakarta to boarding school. And then she missed her parents and Wondemu and the water babies. At night, when she cried, one of her room-mates would have to go get Jakarta. Jakarta would sit on the bed and sing "Barbry Allen" and comb Dakar's hair.

Gingerpuff jumped onto the bed and walked over to knead Dakar's stomach. The cat's eyes, too, seemed drawn to the smoke. All three of them, Dakar thought, were mesmerized by the smoke. She rolled the word *mesmerized* around in her mind, wondering if Jakarta, wherever she was, could really sense that they were thinking about her. Could candle smoke travel all the way to Kenya? What if Jakarta wasn't even *alive* anymore? She scrambled up, brushing the cracker crumbs onto the floor.

"Did you ever find out where the water babies went?" Melanie asked.

It was almost dark outside Melanie's window. What if Jakarta was in big trouble and needed her right this minute? Dakar hadn't even told Mom and Dad where she was. "I've gotta go," she said.

"Wait!" Melanie grabbed her arm.

Dakar pulled away. "I can't wait. I remembered that I need to get home."

"Well, just a second," Melanie said. "Hey, I got this great idea."

Dakar hesitated. The doorknob was burning her hand.

"I think we should have a sleep-over," Melanie said quickly. "That's sort of adventuresome. My grandma gave me a dress-up box, so we could act out one of your stories and everything. What do you think? Saturday?"

"Maybe." How could she have stayed away so long? "I'll ask."

She could tell even before she pushed open the door that the house was too quiet. Her father was reading the newspaper on the couch. "Anything about . . ." The words leaped into her mouth, but saying them would make everything more real. Besides, why would Cottonwood, North Dakota, have any news about Kenya?

Dad was frowning. Dakar tried to breathe. Were his eyes moving on the page? No. She was sure they weren't. He wasn't even reading. "Dad?"

He dropped the newspaper into his lap. She ran

and flopped down on the couch beside him, wishing she could jump onto the newspaper, the way she did when she was little. "Did we hear something?"

"Oh . . . no." He rubbed her cheek. "I'm sorry I scared you. Actually, you scared me when you didn't come home. You should call if you're not going to come home."

Dakar glanced warily at the telephone. She didn't like telephones. There weren't any in Maji or at boarding school, and she never spent much time using the one in Kenya, where ordinary people for some reason never had their names in the phone book and the phone lines were often down or phones disconnected, anyway. But she could probably figure out how to use this one. "Where's Mom?"

"She stayed in bed today. Just resting."

Dakar coughed. It felt as if a small chunk of ice had gotten caught in her lungs. Mom was probably fine, though. She had been unusually cheerful since they came to Cottonwood. "Is she ever going to take a trip to see where she grew up?"

Dad rattled the edge of the paper restlessly. "I have no clue. I thought that was the main reason why we came to North Dakota. She won't talk about it. I don't think anybody understands— including her."

Dakar stared idly at the picture of the family Mom had hung by the table. Dad and Jakarta were laughing, their arms around each other. She herself had her mouth open and was holding up one finger as if to say "wait a second." Mom must have been looking at something off to the side, but you couldn't tell what. "No, you're wrong," she wanted to say. "Someone might understand. Me." But people just didn't go around telling Dad he was wrong. And maybe she didn't even really understand. Still, it seemed to her that Mom might be like a scarab beetle. The ancient Egyptians considered scarab beetles sacred because new beetles seemed to pop mysteriously and miraculously out of little balls of dung. Really, though, adult beetles laid their eggs and then rolled and rolled the dung with their hind legs until the eggs were hidden deep inside.

Maybe Mom had been like that, burying the North Dakota piece of her heart in a neat little ball of ice. Maybe she was afraid of what might happen if she saw the place where she'd grown up. What if seeing it didn't help, and the hard little ball was still there? Or . . . what if she loved it so much that she never wanted to leave North Dakota again?

Dad ran his hand through his graying red hair, making it stick up everywhere. "I was thinking about something that doesn't have anything to do with Jakarta. The doctors in a medical center in Atlanta have been consulting with me about a case that's baffling them. They thought it might be something tropical. I was just going over everything in my mind, wondering what I'm missing. What could I possibly be missing?"

Dakar pulled back. She hated the smell of newspaper. And she hated the person Dad was thinking about. Wait. What a terrible thought! She wanted to care about the patient, a person who was lying in a hospital bed . . . itching, hurting, maybe even dying. I care, she thought quickly. I do care, I do. It's just that there were so many people all the time, always wanting to be near Dad or neeeeding him.

She wished she were more like God and Dad. Mrs. Yoder said, "The Bible suggests that God loves poor people most especially." The first story Dakar ever wrote said, "God loves lepers. My dad loves lepers. But I am scared of them."

Well, okay, her heart definitely wasn't frozen yet, if she could feel guilt. The honest, shameful truth was, she wanted him to be sitting on the couch and thinking about Jakarta, only Jakarta. But she would never say that to him. Dad, who had such a big heart for the wretched and the poor and the sick, would never understand. Besides, ever since boarding school she and Jakarta had been careful about saying anything that would hurt Mom's or Dad's feelings. Every moment with your family was precious. You learned that in boarding school even if you didn't learn anything else.

FOUR

That night in her sleep Dakar quit breathing again. She woke up gasping—huge, noisy gulps. When air was finally trickling back in her lungs, she started to cough.

Through the coughing she heard footsteps. She felt the light in her face. "Dakar?" She felt Dad's hands pulling her up. He held a glass of water to her mouth.

"I'm okay." It was a good sign she could talk, even if she had to croak the words out.

"Don't try to talk. Just breathe calmly."

Breathe calmly. The cough was a crocodile, its eyes sinister above the surface of the water. It wanted to pull her under, but she wouldn't let it. She could still fight back. She made herself breathe in time to the words Mrs. Yoder had taught her: " 'You will not fear the terror of the night.' " In. Out. " 'Nor the arrow that flies by day.' " In. Out. " 'Nor the pestilence that stalks in darkness.' " In. Out. " 'Nor the destruction that wastes at noonday.' " Too bad she did fear all those things, no matter how many times she said the psalm.

"Has this happened to you before?" Dad asked.

"A few times in boarding school. My roommates would run and get Jakarta." Jakarta. Jakarta singing. " 'They climbed and climbed to the steeple top, 'til they could climb no higher. And then they twined in a true lovers' knot—the red rose and the briar.' " Dakar would feel warm and *attached*, knowing that Jakarta was the red rose and she was the briar.

"More than once or twice?" Dad's voice made her a little scared—as if he were mad, though she knew he probably wasn't mad. Just impatient.

"I can't remember." She didn't want to remember. "One of my roommates told Jakarta that sometimes it sounded like I was holding my breath, and this roommate had trouble sleeping, anyway, and she said I made it all the worse because she felt like she had to stay awake and listen in case I . . . you know. So they moved her to another room."

"I wish someone had told us."

He isn't mad, Dakar reminded herself. He just sounds that way. "Jakarta used to sing to me," she whispered.

"Well, lie back. Here, I'll turn out the light, and then I'll sing."

It wasn't "Barbry Allen," but she liked his

songs, and he had a good voice. Such interesting music in the world. The shepherd flutes in Ethiopia. And sometimes in Egypt there were weddings right outside the compound, with wailing Arab music all night. Everyone showed up for class bleary-eyed after nights like that, and tests were postponed. In Nairobi Mom got their cook to teach her some songs in Swahili.

Mom. Dakar sat up. "Where's Mom?"

He stopped in mid-phrase, and she had the discombobulating feeling that they weren't in Cottonwood at all, but out on the African plains together, in the dark. Out there she always knew when he'd heard a dangerous sound, a pestilence that stalks in darkness. She'd lie there with her heart just throbbing.

"Things can get unpredictable out here, fast," he used to tell her. "When I say frog, you jump." She had sat with him in silence like this many times, wondering what was happening, listening to the way his breath whistled in and out. Not asking.

But no. They weren't in Africa. Perhaps pestilence didn't stalk in darkness in quite the same way in Cottonwood, North Dakota. "Never mind," she said. "Now I remember you told me she's been in bed all day. Did she eat any supper?"

"No. But don't worry, Dakar. She'll be fine."

She settled back. Fine. But what if she wasn't? What if—what if the hoodies were after her? When the hoodies pulled Mom into the Allalonestone in Maji, Jakarta knew what to do. Now Dakar would have to figure out how to save Mom. "Don't worry," people always said. "Don't worry." But she *had* to worry. "What's the scariest thing that ever happened to you?"

"Hmm." Dad's fingers found a knot in her left shoulder and kneaded it so hard she wanted to wince, but he liked her to be strong, so she didn't. "Well, I think you were there. Do you remember?"

Of course she remembered. "Don't let your fear get the upper hand. It has a way of swallowing people—whole," Dad had said on that terrible afternoon after the elephant charged them and she was sitting on the ground, more afraid than she could ever remember being in her life (which was saying something), shaking so hard she couldn't move even though an acacia thorn was sticking into her leg.

"I'm okay," she'd said because that was the sort of thing you said to Dad. But she wasn't okay. For months and months she'd felt frozen and sick every time the memory flew back into her mind: the elephant fanning its huge ears, staring straight at her, the trackers with rifles in the ready position, every-one walking carefully backward. At night, just before she fell asleep, she saw herself tripping, falling flat, those sharp tusks coming down.

"It was scary," Dad said, "but when it was over, I could smell every leaf, see every blade of grass. I felt a oneness with the elephant, with everything." He laughed. "I felt gloriously, impossibly alive."

He loved it when things like that happened to him. Why didn't she?

"Well, maybe you'll actually get back to sleep more quickly if I leave."

"No." She grabbed his hand, filled with an immense fear of being alone, utterly alone, the Allalonestone kind of alone where everyone you know has forgotten you and no one will come when you cry or maybe they're even dead and can't come. Where were the words to say what she was feeling? What good was it to be a polyglot if you couldn't find any language to talk about this? "Why did you let me go to boarding school?" she asked because she didn't know what else to say and she didn't want him to go.

"But you wanted to go." Dad's voice was full of surprise. "Mom was the one who kept saying it wasn't a good idea."

Dakar tried to think about whether this was true. She *had* missed Jakarta. That was true.

"Let me rub your back for a minute," Dad said. "We both need to get some sleep."

His hands were strong, and after a few minutes she was drifting. "Did you miss your mom and dad when you were in boarding school?" she whispered.

"All the time," he said. "I miss them now. Your grandparents were people of great faith. They had to be, didn't they? To leave their families, to take a baby halfway across the world and raise him in East Africa? I've often wished I had their faith."

She wanted to say, "Why don't you?" but she didn't want to make him feel bad. Her tight muscles felt like sailor knots under Dad's fingers. He *seemed* to have a lot of faith. He could have been rich if he'd wanted to because when he was studying parasites in graduate school, his parents were killed by parasites, and their insurance company gave Dad money. Lots of money. A lawyer, Mom said, invested it, and Dad never touched it until he was working in Ethiopia and the Centers for Disease Control went through budget cuts. Then he was able to say *kwaheri* to working for institutions. He could go on doing the work that needed to be done. Wasn't that faith?

"I only know two things," Dad said.

His fingers were making her sore muscles hurt, but it was a kind of pain Dakar liked. She also liked it when people put things in numbers that way. It made things easier to hang on to.

"The first thing," he said, "is that I never had my parents' kind of faith. For me, Africa was home, so it never felt scary to choose to live there, even though I'd seen for myself that awful things could happen in a blink."

Dakar shook her head. She wanted him to have faith. She wanted him to say that someone or something was watching over Jakarta. Mrs. Yoder would have said that. Even Melanie's aunt had faith. Oh, Jakarta, she thought suddenly. Are you lost? Please don't be one of the water babies. Please don't be.

"The hell of it," Dad said thoughtfully, "is that even though I didn't inherit their faith, I did inherit a kind of fierce compassion they had. I've ended up with the same compulsion—to make a difference. To leave the world a better place than I found it."

Without any warning he started to laugh. "I guess the one thing I can say for sure is that your mom and I promised each other not to say no to any adventure that came our way, and we're still keeping our promise."

Wait. Was that two things or three? And what if *she* wanted to stop having adventures? Dakar couldn't remember a time when she hadn't been afraid for him. Listening as he told her about meeting the snarling cheetah at dusk. Watching him struggle to hold the grass roof on the clinic in a windstorm. Looking up as he dangled beside a waterfall high above her head. There had to be something better, something safer, than sliding through life like a water baby on a flimsy boat, never stopping anywhere for long.

She was trying to think what to say when she felt his hands pull away from her. She wanted to pull them back. But it was better not to get used to having anyone's hands in the night. Anyway, they all needed to get some sleep. She knew *that* from boarding school. You'd feel better if you could just get the night over with.

"I'll get you warm milk," he whispered. "It will help you sleep."

She would sleep, she thought as his footsteps died away. She would sleep—because it would be too awful to lie there awake. In boarding school she would sometimes say the books of the Bible. Genesis, Exodus, Leviticus, Numbers, Deuteronomy, Joshua, Judges, Ruth . . . oops. She hadn't said them for a while, and now she was stuck. How about the former Russian czars, since she was reading about them in social studies? Alexander I, Alexander II, Alexander III, Boris Godunov. Wait. Boris was before the Alexanders. She could feel it all starting to jumble in her mind. Boris Godunov JoshuaJudgesRuth . . .

She woke up at least two more times that night. The first time she was pretty sure she heard Dad yelling something. But maybe she wasn't really awake because she could also clearly smell that huge permanent puddle of gray water and old motor oil, and that puddle covered the street outside their apartment in Egypt.

Even later she vaguely thought she heard a phone ringing. "Yes?" Was that her father shouting, or was it in her dream? "Yes?" A few minutes later he was at her door. "Are you awake? It's okay. I got in touch with an old friend in Frankfurt who happened to be in e-mail contact with someone in the Sudan who had a shortwave radio contact in Nairobi. That person let the school know to put Jakarta on the next plane. It'll still be a few days, but the school said she's fine."

What about the quest? Dakar thought sleepily. She hadn't even had a chance to save Jakarta. Suddenly she was wide awake and feeling foolish. Then it struck her. Maybe she *had* gone on a quest without even knowing it. Was it possible the banister was the first brave thing and the high school door was the second and the cook was the third? And what about the candle smoke or making a true friend? Maybe she'd heard Jakarta's voice because she'd made some kind of eerie connection. Wouldn't that be weird? She'd have to ask Jakarta when she got home.

She reached out for the glass by her bedside table. Ugh. The milk was cold. She could warm it up if she could figure out how to work the microwave. Instead, she snuggled under the blanket, hugging her pillow. She stared into the darkness, trying to connect her mind to Jakarta's. As she finally drifted off, two thoughts blazed through her mind, one right after the other.

The first was, Jakarta is coming home.

The second was, Now everything will be perfect.

□   □   □

*True stories of mysterious and unexplained
things I know about personally*

1. Mom heard Grandma's voice after Grandma was dead.

2. After being this incredibly important thing to the children of Israel, the Ark of the Covenant suddenly disappears from the Bible. Where did it go? Is it hidden somewhere in Ethiopia? A lot of Ethiopians believe it is. I know King Solomon's Ethiopian son couldn't really have flown through the air when he was stealing the Ark, the way the story says. But Dad says the legends could have sprung out of real true facts.

3. In a museum in Cairo there is something made out of sycamore wood that looks totally like a glider. Where would the ancient Egyptians have seen something like that? Also, I've seen some ancient Egyptian carvings on the temple wall at Abydos, and I can tell you they look like airplanes and helicopters.

4. Even scientists can't figure out how the pyramids were really made. Or the giant obelisks that are a thousand years old that we saw at

Axum in Ethiopia. Or how those huge churches at Lalibela could have been carved out of stone—inside and out—in the eleventh or twelfth century. The Ethiopians say that angels helped. Did they?

5. When we were camping at Lake Naivasha, Dad told us scary stories by Edgar Allan Poe. One was "The Tell-Tale Heart" and the other was "The Pit and the Pendulum." Then he said, I'll tell you a true story. Poe wrote a story about some shipwrecked sailors who killed and ate a cabin boy named Richard Parker. Fifty years later some real shipwrecked sailors killed and ate a man named Richard Parker. Dad said that's called synchronicity. He said some people think stuff like that is an incredible coincidence, but the guy named Jung who made up the word thought the universe was made up of patterns too complicated for humans to understand and everything is all linked together in mysterious ways.

6. Mom has had synchronicity happen to her. When she had just graduated from college, she was reading a *National Geographic* about Indonesia and decided that was where she wanted to go more than anyplace in the world. That after-

noon she was at her job as a waitress in Nowhere, North Dakota, and she started talking with an interesting-looking stranger who ordered ham and eggs in the middle of the afternoon. It turned out he had gotten lost on his way to a place where he was supposed to interview teachers for a school in Indonesia.

7. The quest I went on in Maji with Jakarta. Did we really rescue Mom from the hoodies and the Allalonestone?

FIVE

The best thing about the next morning was Mom pushing the hair out of Dakar's eyes and looking right at her with astonishingly blue eyes. Mom saying, "Dakar! You need to eat breakfast before you go to school."

"I love it when you boss me around," Dakar said, truly happy. "Will you fix me pancakes? Please please please?"

There were soft shadows under Mom's eyes, but otherwise she looked strong. The Allalonestone hoodies—*if* they'd even really had hold of Mom again—had definitely let go. They weren't going to pull Mom under this time. "Maybe Saturday for pancakes," she said. "Or how about the first morning Jakarta is back? Remember when I used to make you birthday pancakes? When Jakarta comes home, it'll be as good as a birthday, won't it?"

"Better." Dakar hugged Mom, remembering those birthday mornings, the candles melting on top of a stack of whole wheat pancakes. She and Jakarta had gotten the idea from a book. What book? Jakarta would know.

Unfortunately birthday mornings came in boarding school, too. At the end of the month everyone got to sit at a birthday table and have everyone sing, but it wasn't the same. Jakarta always pulled her aside, though, between the dorm and school and slipped a candy bar into her hand, something special saved from store night two weeks before.

Mom touched Dakar's forehead again, almost shyly. "When did you start to wear your hair that way? It makes you look more like Jakarta, except hers isn't red, of course."

"I know." Dakar flexed one of her skinny arms and made a muscle. "I'm getting buff like her, too." *Buff* was a great new word she got from Melanie. "But I wish you would call my hair auburn."

Mom laughed. "Okay. Not as red as your dad's. Though I've always thought you looked like him."

Dakar felt absurdly happy, as though she'd just been told she resembled God. "But my eyes aren't like his." Dad's eyes were deep brown. Her eyes were blue. Not Mom's blue. Just blue. "And he doesn't have freckles."

Mom smoothed Dakar's bridge of freckles with both thumbs. "I'll bet he did when he was twelve. If his mom or dad were still alive, we could ask."

The next best thing about the day was being able to say yes to Melanie's Saturday plan. Why not? By the time they were walking to school together, Dakar felt expansive, full of goodwill. Goodwill. Just thinking the word made her laugh.

" 'Fear not,' " she said to Melanie, spreading her arms and pretending that she had great, shimmering wings to flap. " 'For behold I bring you good tidings of great joy. Peace on earth and goodwill to all' . . . to all human beings."

"Whoa," Melanie said. "Including the hockey players?" They giggled together, and Dakar felt she might grow real wings and start floating. She put her hand against her chest. No ice in there today. The glow had melted it all.

Except—except that Melanie's comment had started worries bubbling again. She'd never seen a hockey game or a football game. How stupid was that going to seem? And what *was* Jakarta going to play here? "It's all right," she told herself. Jakarta had to be happy that the four of them would be together again. "I just remembered I've got to do something," Dakar said. "It's urgent." Without waiting for Melanie to answer, she started to run. She had to be sure she had enough time to get downstairs before the first bell rang.

"Africa child," the cook said before she could say anything. "You are full of glory today. The heavens are telling the glory of God, as my mother used to say to each one of her children every single morning."

"What about that day to day pours forth speech part?" Dakar asked. "Don't you like that? Good storytellers pour forth speech, don't you think? I know I feel that way when I'm telling one of my favorite stories."

The cook clicked her tongue. "Your parents surely did bring you up to know your good word, Africa child. Or did the Bible just come bubbling up out of the hot springs over there?"

Dakar laughed. "Neither," she said. "And I wanted to tell you that my big sister is coming home. That's why I look so full of glory."

"Your sister." The cook let out a long, squeaky sigh. "Well, you know, *that's* a hallelujah moment, Africa child. I do wish I could see my own sister. There's a wide, wide ocean between me and my baby sister."

"Why don't you go see her?" Dakar asked.

The cook shook her head. "I was born saying I would never, ever get up in an airplane. Then life twisted itself around me, and up I went in spite of all I had to say." She chuckled. "And isn't that life? But when God set me safely down on North Dakota solid ground, I vowed that was my last airplane flight. No, I think these willing ears will never be hearing my beloved baby sister pouring forth speech again."

At the door Dakar hesitated. "About the Bible," she said. "I went to a boarding school for a while where they thought Memory Work was very important. Mrs. Yoder would write the verses on Holy Cards and make us practice. What if you were on a desert island sometime, she would say to us, or in a prison cell? If you have the words in your heart, no one can take them away."

"Uh-huh," the cook was saying as Dakar turned. "It all pretty much comes down to what's in your heart."

On her way up the stairs Dakar thought about what the cook had said. It probably all pretty much did come down to what was in your heart. But it was so terribly, terribly hard to have a pure heart. She should care more about the people Dad was finding cures for, for example. The truly true truth was that she was mad at them at least half the time. Because it seemed like Dad spent so much time with them, and when he wasn't with someone who had some strange disease, he was thinking about them.

"This is the second time you've been late, Dakar," Ms. Olson said as she walked in the door. "Second time is supposed to be detention."

Dakar swallowed. She wasn't the kind of student to be late to class, and she'd never, ever had detention.

Ms. Olson was frowning. "Every once in a while my mom gets really sick," Dakar said. Well, it wasn't an actual lie, was it? "Sometimes she doesn't know that she's going to need me, but then I can't really leave until someone else is there to stay with her. I'm sorry."

Don't give me detention, she thought. How embarrassing did life have to get? She concentrated on looking contrite. What a good word that was. She knew she didn't have a pure heart, but she surely had a *contrite* one.

"See me if you need help getting it worked out," Ms. Olson said. "It's an important middle school responsibility to get to classes on time."

Dakar scowled at the kids who had turned around to look. Contriteness had helped again. Or maybe it was only that all the teachers here had probably been warned, "She's from Africa. She doesn't know the things normal kids know."

Sixth grade in the United States was harder than she'd expected. The classes were bigger than she was used to. Plus, the sixth grade had just become part of Cottonwood Middle School this year. "We have to be tough," teachers said these first days when kids complained about anything. "We have to get you used to the system. Otherwise, you'll never make it next year." Were the teachers going to say that every year from now on?

Dakar didn't dare pull out her lists and thoughts book today, not having just escaped detention. Instead, she doodled on the side of her paper, little hoodies with frightening eyes. She gave one hoodie a talk balloon. *"Ferenji,"* it was saying. That was "foreigner" in Ethiopia. Not that the little kids who yelled it every time she walked down the Maji road were mean like the hoodies, but she still didn't like hearing them say *ferenji* over and over or having them pinch her skin to see what it was made of. In Kenya, the word was *mzungu*. In Egypt people said *khawaaga*, with one of those growling sounds that were so fun to say in Arabic.

What was the word going to be here in Cottonwood? Thinking about the hockey and football games, Dakar was sure it would be something. Which was weird, because wasn't she supposed to be home? That morning in Nairobi Mom had said, "I can't believe we're really going home." Lots of people in Africa said things like "We'll be going home for the year" when they meant the United States of America. Dakar couldn't remember when she had first started thinking that the little frozen spots that sometimes popped up in her stomach and lungs would go away if she could just get home. So why were the spots still there?

"Jakarta's coming home," Dakar whispered to herself, and instantly felt better, even though the day crept along and she had to keep trying to think of things to do to keep from dying of impatience. By the time she got to math class, she was writing numbers the way her Egyptian friends wrote them. The numbers looked quite a bit like American numbers, but different in a cool, poetic way. She remembered practicing her numbers on a train in Egypt sitting beside Jakarta and watching mile-posts whip by. They had just said good-bye to Mom and Dad, who were going to go off and have an adventure together, and the numbers helped her keep from crying.

Oops. She hadn't heard a word of math class. She

looked up quickly. "You are the engineers of the world's future," Mr. Johnson was saying. "You need to have a good foundation in math because it's going to be up to you to fix the world's pollution and other problems." Dakar drew a scowling hoodie face. It was a good thing Jakarta would be here soon. Jakarta was interested in being an engineer of the world's future. Jakarta thought about that kind of stuff.

She shifted on the chair. Now what would make positive and negative integers go *fast*? Whole numbers were comforting. What was scary was realizing that between any two whole numbers was an infinity of fractions and other things that made everything too dizzifying and unpredictable. When it came to infinity, all the peace on earth and goodwill could only go so far.

SIX

When Melanie met Dakar at the door on Saturday, the first thing she said was, "Do you know sign language?"

Dakar shook her head. "Not even one word."

"Everybody in the whole world knows 'I love you.' " Melanie showed Dakar. "One of my aunts is taking a class because she's going to be a teacher. She's teaching me a bunch of other words." She signed again. "Know what I just said? 'Help me. I'm a buttery potato on fire.' "

"If I was a potato," Dakar said, "I'd want to be a buttery potato."

"If I was a butterfly," Melanie said, "I'd want to be an empress butterfly."

"If I had to be a butterfly," Dakar said, "I'd want to be a big strong blue one." Melanie was staring at her with a look of fascination. "If I had to be a pizza," she added, laughing, "I'd be a greasy one with cheese sliding off in six different directions."

Melanie made a magnificent leap toward her room. "Inside the magic room," she said, "we can be anything we want. Hurry." So Dakar hurried. Melanie had put a gauzy purple scarf over the lamp so the room was lit in dim softness. Some kind of incense burning filled the room with a smell of black silk and yellow amber. Melanie pulled a green cowboy hat out of the box in the middle of the room.

"Huzzah," Dakar said dryly.

Next, Melanie pulled out a scarf from a box and draped it around her head, making a veil. "Is this more like it?"

"It definitely fits my stories better," Dakar said. "I could think of one to go with that."

"Cool." Melanie plopped on the bed. "I knew it. I just *knew* it."

Dakar looked into Melanie's eyes, which blinked over the top of the veil. "Okay, I'll tell you a story from Somalia. I've never been there. Too dangerous. But usually when my dad comes home from anywhere, he tells me stories."

"Why did he go to Somalia?"

"Some medical thing." Dakar tried to remember if he had ever told them, exactly. People desperately needing help. War probably. There were always so many sad true stories.

"Where all have you lived?" Melanie asked.

Dakar settled herself into storytelling position on the chair, back straight, legs crossed. "In West Africa until I was three. I don't remember that at all. In Egypt when I was four. I think I remember Egypt, but we lived there again when I was ten, so maybe I'm really remembering that. In Maji the longest—five to seven. I went to boarding school in Addis Ababa when I was eight and nine and only went home to Maji at Christmas and in the summer."

"Wow," Melanie said. "How could you stand not seeing your mom and dad for so long?"

Dakar shrugged. "It was hard. Egypt when I was ten. Dad was in Somalia. Nairobi when I was eleven and Dad spent a lot of time in the Sudan. Now I'm twelve and I'm here."

"I thought you'd be eleven, like me," Melanie said.

"I'm used to being the oldest in my class. Mom says I was always small for my age, and she home-schooled me for the first two years, so she didn't want to push."

"No wonder you're so mature for your age. Here, put this on." Melanie tossed a bracelet to Dakar. "It's the most exotic thing I have. My aunt got it at the Wisconsin Dells."

Dakar fastened it. "You have to be absolutely quiet so I can start." Feeling powerful and dramatic, she held up her arms. The bracelet gleamed. Dakar took a deep breath. The beginnings of stories were probably the most important parts to get right.

"Long ago in the grasslands of Somalia lived a man who was chief of a mighty clan, so rich he had a thousand camels. The man loved his camels and his horses, his sheep and his goats, but more, far more, he loved his daughter, Donbirra, who was graceful as a leopard." She was relieved to discover she hadn't forgotten anything. She'd loved this story from the first time Dad told it. She loved "graceful as a leopard." She loved it that Donbirra's father loved her more than anything in the world. "Nothing was too good for Donbirra," she went on. "She always had hippopotamus hide sandals for her feet and amber beads to hang around her neck."

"Wait," Melanie said. "I'm sure we can find the hippopotamus hide sandals in here." She rummaged, giggling.

"Year after year," Dakar said, not waiting, "the man and his daughter and his clan moved with the rains, following the water." Then there was this terrific place, when the story started to flow, the words blossoming out of her mouth like fancy, flapping butterflies. Fat, smooth words she could almost taste.

Melanie abandoned the box. "Go on," she said. She sat on the floor and stared up at Dakar.

"Okay. Well, when the Dhair rains were few and water was scarce, they settled by a river. There the young men drove the camels out to find grass. And there Donbirra watched the sheep and goats and made rope, and in the evening she took smoke baths of myrrh and frankincense."

"I knew it," Melanie said triumphantly. "The smell in this room is perfect, isn't it?"

"Day followed peaceful day," Dakar went on. "But one day a mighty noise shook the camp. When the chief stepped out from under his awning of palm branches and went to see what was happening, he found three young men standing in the middle of his camp.

"Two of the men were dressed in new clothes with ostrich feathers in their hair and ivory bracelets on their arms. By this the man knew they were great warriors. The first stepped forward and lifted his shield of rhinoceros hide. 'We have heard of your wonderful daughter,' he said.

"The second stepped forward and shook his spear. Then he said, 'Do you give me your daughter?'

"The chief looked at Donbirra where she sat with her sheep and goats, but he saw no softness in her eyes when she looked at the warriors. So he said, 'But there are two of you. If I choose one and not the other, I may offend your father who will come and do me harm. And what about this third?'

"The oldest brother laughed. 'This son of a hyena? He is our youngest brother, Jama. He never fights but plays his shepherd's pipe all day and half the night. We brought him along to carry our things.'

"The father looked thoughtful. 'I cannot choose,' he said. 'Give me time to think.' "

"How come he gets to choose, anyway?" Melanie asked.

"Well, what am I supposed to do?" Dakar said. "Change the story because we don't happen to think that's the right way to do things? My dad always says we have to meet people where they are. He also says, 'Just be quiet and listen to what people have to tell you about their lives.' "

She paused. Did it make Donbirra mad or did it make her feel loved? Daughters of chiefs and kings couldn't reveal their feelings. They had to be secretive to survive. Did Alexander I and Alexander II and those other Russian czars have princess daughters? Why didn't school teach you the important things, like whether the daughters ever got to choose and how they felt when their fathers were off solving the important problems of Russia.

"Anyway, in the days that followed," she went on, "Donbirra's father consulted the Koran and talked to the *wadad*, who was always wise. Every day the brothers came to him and asked him to make his choice. Every day Donbirra's father looked at his daughter, but her eyes were cool and smooth as eggshells as she watched the warriors. So he said, 'I cannot choose.' The brothers walked by the river, waving their spears and talking. As for Jama, he played his flute so sweetly that Donbirra's sheep and goats seemed to smile as they grazed.

"Finally, one day when the brothers came to the man, he said, 'I still cannot choose. But the *wadad* has made a suggestion. Tomorrow we will begin a contest to see which of you is most worthy to marry my daughter.'

"Next day, when the morning sun was hot in the sky, all the people gathered. 'Now,' the chief said to the first brother, 'what do you have to show us?'

"The first brother stepped forward. First he boasted of the many battles he had fought. Then he lifted his spear. He took a silver coin from his pouch and tossed it high in the air. For a moment

it spun. Then the warrior hurled his spear. *Whoosh.*
The spear pierced the silver coin while it was still
spinning. The people cried out. The chief nodded
in admiration. But when he looked at Donbirra,
she was laughing at Jama, who had charmed some
monkeys into throwing their fruit to him."

Dakar looked at Melanie. She could tell Melanie
was wanting to ask something, but when Dakar
frowned, Melanie clamped her hand obediently
over her mouth. "If you want to know where he got
a silver coin, I don't know," Dakar said. "They had
silver coins in Ethiopia before Jesus was born,
even. Maybe they have in Somalia, too. So, back to
the story.

"Donbirra's father sighed. 'I cannot choose. Go
back to your tents, and we shall continue the contest tomorrow.'

"All that evening he weighed one stone in his
hand and then another. He consulted with the eld-
ers and muttered and thought, thought and muttered. As for Donbirra, she helped Jama teach the
milk camels how to dance.

"When the next day was golden with sun, the
crowd again gathered. The people laughed and
argued together, favoring first one brother and
then the other. Finally the second warrior stepped

forward. First he boasted of how fierce he was in battle. Then he said, 'Look. With my spear I can take the twig that the boy over there holds between his teeth.'

"The boy stopped chewing and stood up. All the people watched. Almost before they could breathe, the spear shot through the air and knocked the small stick right out of the boy's mouth.

"The crowd clicked their tongues in awe. The chief looked at Donbirra. But she picked up her water jug and started down to the river to get water. 'I cannot choose,' the chief muttered. The warriors shuffled impatiently.

"Suddenly two eyes rose up out of the river like bush fruits, and the water began to ripple. Just as Donbirra lifted her full water jug from the river, a crocodile sprang half out of the water, twisting its head sideways to open its mouth."

Melanie gave a satisfying gasp.

"Donbirra leaped back," Dakar said dramatically. "The crocodile's mouth crashed shut, catching the corner of Donbirra's *maro*. With a cry Donbirra dropped the jar.

" 'Your spears,' the chief shouted to the warriors. 'Throw your spears.'

"But the oldest brother said, 'In my clan only

slaves and outcasts hunt animals. It would be beneath me to kill a beast.'

" 'For me it is just the same,' the second brother said.

"No one noticed Jama running toward the river. The crocodile opened its huge mouth again." Dakar moved her arms wide apart to show the crocodile jaws, just the way Dad would if he were telling the story. "Donbirra fell backward against the bank. The crocodile's teeth flashed in the sun.

"Then Jama was there. Kneeling close to the crocodile and putting his flute to his lips, he began to play. The music tickled the leaves of the tamarisk tree and set the goats frisking in the grass. Slowly the crocodile closed its mouth. Then it slid back into the river and rolled over and over in the water, rippling bubbles as it went."

Dakar paused for just the right moment. "As for Donbirra," she said triumphantly, "perhaps the music charmed her also. In any case, her eyes, as she looked at Jama, were soft as moonlight on leaves. And when Jama stood before the chief and asked, 'Do you give me your daughter?' the chief smiled and called to his people, 'Let us all celebrate. May the feasts begin. At last I think I can choose.' "

Melanie sighed and flopped back. "How romantic," she said. "Even if the dad did get to think he was choosing. Or do you think he knew?" She didn't wait for an answer. "Isn't it cool that we're having a sleep-over? I can't believe that I'm sleeping in the same room with someone who has slept in Africa. The most exciting thing I've done until now was wearing socks that don't match."

Dakar closed her eyes. She had done such a good job telling the story. She could just imagine the audience clapping and clapping. *Thunderous* applause, the books always said. But tonight something about the story made her sad. Something about Dad. It wasn't that Dad would ever choose anything important for her. He was too big into JUSTICE, with capital letters. But would Dad study her eyes, trying to see if there was any softness in them? No, he would be busy thinking about something much more important, like finding a cure for river blindness.

"Tell me something you really, really remember from Africa," Melanie said.

Dakar slid off the chair with her eyes still closed and balanced on one leg like the tall warriors she used to stare at, fascinated by their blue-black skin and their clay hairdos. Where should she start?

Could she make the exact sound the lizards made when they woke her up in the morning, sliding down the tin roof? Could she explain about mornings Jakarta was gone, when Dakar scrambled up the hill to the village through a lion's mane of fog, the lion's tongue licking her all over, leaving her dripping wet? The sweet mist of eucalyptus smoke over the town? The thicker, warmer smoke smell inside Wondemu's house, and Wondemu's grandmother leaning over to hand her a fat, fleshy banana for breakfast?

She opened her eyes. "I don't know," she said. "I live here now. Let's dig through the box, okay?"

SEVEN

Sunday morning Dakar woke up with princesses dancing in her head, and she couldn't get them out, even though Melanie's mom served omelets for breakfast. Where did Melanie get her genes from? Dakar looked back and forth between the two of them as they bent over a catalog. Melanie's mom had broad shoulders and a generous, practical face. Melanie was like a river sprite, delicate and small with almost white hair and river-colored eyes. Maybe she was a changeling. A jinn baby.

As if she had read Dakar's mind, Melanie looked up and gave her an elfin grin. "Come on," she whispered into Dakar's ear. "I want to show you the most magical spot in Cottonwood. I've never showed anybody else."

"What would you do," Dakar said as they started to walk, "if you were a princess trapped in a high tower, and an evil hen gave you three impossible tasks you had to solve or you could never, ever get out and go home?"

"Well, what would the tasks be?" Melanie asked.

"One would be to turn that tree over there into a pomegranate tree," Dakar said. "And the next would be to pick a pomegranate from the very heart of the tree and count its seeds."

"First, she'd have to know what a pomegranate was," Melanie said.

"Well, she'd know that," Dakar said impatiently. "All princesses do." She imagined that she was holding a pomegranate seed lightly between her front teeth. She loved the way the seeds felt—all smooth and self-contained—just before you bit. Just before that sweet and bitter pomegranate taste came into your mouth.

The third task would be to find the three magic seeds and take them with her on her quest once she got out of the tower. What if the princess failed at her tasks? Then she would be frozen. The cold would creep upward, starting at her feet. Or downward, starting at the top of her head. Either way, when it reached her heart, she would be done for. Maybe the princess had to find a true friend. Only a true friend would know the answer to the pomegranate problem. Melanie could be the true friend.

"I love that story you told last night," Melanie

said. "It's so perfect that you're not from here. And it's so obvious. Because people from here don't talk in paragraphs. I wish you would tell me more about Jakarta."

Jakarta! "She's incredibly smart," Dakar said. "If she were the princess in the tower, the evil hen wouldn't be able to hold her more than a few hours at most."

"Why?" Melanie said. "How would she get out?"

Dakar kicked a stone down the sidewalk and wondered if she'd be able to pick out that same exact stone when they caught up with it again. It seemed terribly important that she recognize it. "I don't know," she said. "I'm not nearly as smart as Jakarta. Oh, also, she's beautiful. She's like Donbirra. Boys fight their way through dark and miry bogs to touch the edge of her cloak. And she's a soccer star."

"Will she like me?" Melanie asked.

"Sure." Dakar bent down to study the pile of rocks. If she could find the exact stone, what she had just said would be true. Jakarta would like it here. "Thanks for coming on ahead of me," Jakarta would say. "I'm eternally grateful." There. That was the stone. Wasn't it? Dakar felt a flutter of panic. "Stop it," she told herself. You made that test up. There is no evil hen. Switch off the imagination. How long would it take Jakarta to fly back to the U.S.? "You know," Dakar said, "I think I should go home."

"Hey! We were going to the magic place."

"Oh, right." Dakar started to trot. "We have to go quickly, though. I should go home and see if they've got Jakarta's plane schedule yet."

"It's on my uncle's land," Melanie said, hurrying to catch up. "I always knew it was magic, but I didn't have anyone else who would know, too."

Melanie's uncle's land was on the edge of town, and they both were panting by the time they got to it. Melanie pointed to a house but shook her head. She steered them into a grove of trees.

Dakar looked up. Above her head, leaves flickered as if they were candle flames and the wind were trying to blow them out. Trees in Cottonwood were mostly shaped the way Jakarta had first taught her to draw a tree with a fat crayon—two lines, curved at the bottom, and a round top. It made them look friendly and old. Okay, not as old as the old frangapani tree she and Jakarta had loved to visit. But a lot older than the feathery jacaranda trees Yusef had just planted in the Nairobi yard.

If only this magic grove were full of eucalyptus trees. She'd climbed the boarding school eucalyptus trees with Jakarta at least a hundred times, always pretending she wasn't afraid, hoping the skinny branches were as tough as they seemed to be, imagining Jakarta was a red rose and she was a briar. But maybe Melanie's leaves would actually fall off when the weather got cold, the way leaves did in books. They looked green and sturdy, but she could see dabs of interesting colors at the other end of the grove.

"This way," Melanie said, "for the mysterious, magical place."

A creek ran through the grove. Tree roots, from a tree growing close to the water, stuck out from the bank, their twisted arms forming ledges and little caves. "Cool." Dakar scrambled up to sit on a root. It was like sitting on the back of a snake.

"*Très* cool." Melanie scratched her back against the trunk of one of the big trees. "Is this the kind of place where an Allalonestone would be? Or is the Allalonestone a real thing in Africa?"

Dakar hesitated. She and Jakarta were the only ones in the whole world who knew about the Allalonestone. But Jakarta had never said don't tell anyone else, had she?

"There's no such thing as an Allalonestone," she said. "I did used to think it was real, though. Jakarta told me about the hoodies that caught people and forced them inside the Allalonestone. Once you were in there, nothing would get you out. Almost nothing."

"Maybe it's over there." Melanie pointed to a rock jutting out from the creek, shiny with wetness. "Beware of the Allalonestone."

"No." Dakar shivered. "I think it's huge and flat, and the water runs over it. At first, I think even Jakarta halfway believed in the Allalonestone." She remembered running through trees near Maji. "Look," Jakarta was calling to her. "That tree has beards hanging from it. Those are hoodie beards." Looking up at the mossy beards, Dakar walked right into something sticky. She'd screamed and pawed at her face, sure the hoodies must have left a thin ghost film all over everything to catch people and take them to the Allalonestone. But the sticky stuff was only a huge spiderweb.

Should she tell Melanie about the time Mom disappeared? Should she say, "I have this terrible memory of pushing on Mom's door, whimpering"? Should she tell about Jakarta's strong hands pulling her behind the woodstove? Jakarta whispering,

"The hoodies have got Mom, but don't worry. We'll get her back." And they had, hadn't they?

No, she couldn't tell that. Some things were way too personal even for true friendship. But this was a magical place, worthy of secrets. Maybe she could share a little part of it, anyway. She took a deep breath. "I thought Mom was stuck in the Allalonestone once." She glanced at Melanie. Melanie was staring at her with an open mouth. "Dad was off on one of his adventures," she went on, trying to make her voice not jump even the least little bit. "So Jakarta had to take care of me. We did quests together, and one day Jakarta got the idea of making up an incantation."

Dakar was afraid to look at Melanie again. She stooped down and stirred her finger in the creek water. "I don't think the incantation had real power or anything," she said quickly. "But one day we went on what Jakarta called a specially brave quest and then said the incantation. And—here's the weirdest thing—the very minute we stopped saying it, Mom walked out of her room."

Dakar felt a little sick to hear the words that had come out of her mouth. Even at boarding school she had never told anyone about the Allalonestone or the incantation. She didn't have to look at

Melanie to know that Melanie was waiting, waiting to hear the incantation.

Don't think. She straightened up. Don't think. Be brave.

"Fierce!" Melanie whispered. "A real *African* incantation?"

"I guess." Dakar squeezed her mind, trying to remember. "At least, the day it started, Jakarta was wearing a camel bone necklace. But she had just read me an American book that had something about *eye of newt* in it. She said, 'Monkey toe, camel bones, petals of lotus, three,' and the rest just seemed to come magically to her after that. Here. Say it after me. Monkey toe."

"Monkey toe," Melanie repeated obediently.

"Camel bones. Petals of lotus, three. Elephant tusk. Hair of dog. Bark of sycamore tree."

"What's a sycamore tree?" Melanie asked.

"I'm not sure. But I think Jakarta got it from the Bible. Anyway, it just sounds good. Okay. Second verse. Wing of eel."

"But eels don't have wings," Melanie said.

"I know." Dakar fought back her impatience. She never should have started this, but now she had to go on. "Still, that's how the incantation goes. Wing of eel. Tooth of snail. Golden lion's mane. Giraffe's eyelash. Murmur of bat. Three silver birds flying home in the rain."

"The last line doesn't exactly fit."

"I know," Dakar said. "But Jakarta said it was too delicious not to use. Besides, we had just looked up and really seen three birds." She paused. "You must never, ever tell anyone this incantation." She hoped her voice was solemn and scary enough to get through. "Up until this very moment it's something only Jakarta and I knew. Now you know it, too."

"I don't even think I remember it all," Melanie said. "Can we practice some more?"

"First, you have to promise." Dakar tapped Melanie's arm. "You have to give your most solemn, oathful promise not to tell anyone. And then you have to teach me how to sign, okay?"

"Sure," Melanie said. "I can teach you that easily. Here's how you say, 'Are you okay?' Here's how you say, 'Fine.' Here's how you say, 'Fancy fine.' " She giggled.

Dakar refused to laugh. "We can only say the incantation when we're here in this magical place," she said sternly. "And we have to hurry. I can't wait to find out if Mom and Dad know when Jakarta's getting in."

□   □   □

That night Dakar couldn't sleep even though she went all the way to Habakkuk, Zephaniah, Haggai, Zechariah, Malachi. The ancient poetry in the names wasn't working. She gave up and tried Ivan IV, Theodore I, Boris Godunov, Theodore II, False Dimitri . . . she felt a stab of guilt. She had to quit being such a False Dimitri. It was getting to be a bad habit. Ummm . . . Peter I, Catherine I, Peter II, Anne, Ivan VI, Elizabeth, Peter III . . . okay . . . who was next? Alexander I? No, she was missing someone. Or maybe more than one. Sophia ruled while Peter I and Ivan V were children, so Ivan must be with Peter. Which Catherine was Catherine the Great? Dakar didn't feel any closer to sleep than before she had started.

Think about something else. Think about Jakarta coming. Tuesday afternoon, Mom said. That was day after tomorrow. Tuesday afternoon. Tuesday afternoon, Tuesday afternoon, Tuesday afternoon. Over and over Dakar saw it, saw Jakarta coming through the door, saw herself running—running swiftly and lightly as only a princess could—to *fling* her arms around Jakarta. Someday she would tell Jakarta about her quest idea and see what Jakarta thought. Also, she would see if Jakarta had felt anything that moment Dakar heard her voice. But in the airport they would simply twine together, right there in the lounge or on the steps, and vow to never live whole continents away from each other again. The red rose and the briar.

EIGHT

D akar expected to feel gloriously excited when she woke up on Tuesday, but instead, she felt queasy. She wished she hadn't told Melanie about the hoodies and the Allalonestone. "What's the big deal?" she asked herself, rummaging around inside her brain for an answer. But she didn't find one. Only that she was really good at keeping secrets and she didn't have much experience telling secrets. "Do I have to go to school?" she asked at breakfast. "My stomach doesn't feel so great."

Mom's face was shiny hopeful. "You're probably just excited, like me," she said dreamily. "We should make a big sign. KARIBU, JAKARTA."

"Too embarrassing," Dakar said.

"Too embarrassing," Dad agreed. "Why don't you just stay home? Jakarta's flight comes in at one, anyway."

"We should do a project," Mom said, "to make the time go fast. Take a look at the hedge. I haven't had a hedge since I left North Dakota twenty-five years ago, but isn't it supposed to be neater than that? It looks awfully scraggly compared to the neighbor's side of it."

"I have a conference call with the president of the American Society of Tropical Medicine at the university this morning. Then I'll be back." Dad stood up, scooped up Mom's hair, and kissed the back of her neck. "And I like wild hedges. Isn't it bad enough that we're living in a town with square lawns and in a white two-story house? A neat, square hedge, too? Too conventional."

Mom smiled. "Too conventional." After Dad had gone, though, she said to Dakar, "I'll bet we could figure out how to clip that hedge. Let's go see if we can find some tools in the garage."

They made a good team, Dakar thought. She liked the softness of the sunshine, here, and the smooth *schick, schick* of the clippers.

Mom often got this strange look on her face when they were traveling and had gotten absolutely lost and were whirling around one roundabout after another on the wrong side of the road or walking down winding brick streets that all looked the same. Or sometimes it would happen in some airport where people abruptly started shouting and pushing, but no one seemed to speak English. Dad would usually be laughing. Occasionally he'd be yelling. But Mom would get a pained expression as if a big animal were sniffing at her, and if she could stand or sit utterly still, it would go away and not gobble her up. The look always made Dakar's own thoughts start fluttering. What if they stayed lost forever? What if they missed the plane? What if they got kidnapped by someone assuming they were rich Americans? What if they didn't know some custom and people sneered or scowled or laughed?

Out here in the sunshine, Mom's face looked so opposite. She had an expression that was even sort of *exquisite*. "You like it here, don't you?" Dakar said.

Mom smiled. "It's unbelievable. When I think how determined and desperate I was to get out of North Dakota . . . I never expected it to feel so much like home." She added, "When your dad was in second grade, his family came back to the United States to live for a year. He was supposed to take some kind of standardized test to see if his schoolwork was up to grade level. The only thing he remembers about the test is that it had a picket fence on it, and he didn't know what a picket fence was. The woman who was giving him the test had to take him outside to show him one."

Dakar thought about fences. In Maji a fence made of thorn branches surrounded their house and the clinic. Outside the fence were wild pig paths, the waterfalls, and the water babies. She wasn't sure she knew what a picket fence looked like, either.

"When he told me that," Mom said, "he said he never wanted to see another picket fence." She laughed. "We'd just been snorkeling in the turquoise sea. He and I promised each other right there not to say no to any adventure that came our way." She sighed. "So why am I having longings for a white house and a picket fence? Like the one I grew up in. Uf-dah, how your dad would yelp to hear me say that."

Dakar laughed at the funny word. "When can we go there?" she asked. "I want to see where you grew up."

Mom lifted the clippers above her head as though she were preparing to clip the sky. "Well, it's a very long, boring drive across North Dakota," she said flatly. "But I do keep meaning to write to Aunt Lily. It would sure be easier if she had a phone, but maybe . . ." She let the clippers slowly drop. "Oh, well," she said, "most longings pass."

Dakar glanced up at the house. It was awfully sedate compared with the places they usually lived. Dad seemed to give off an energy that pulled people right in, and when he was home, their house in Nairobi was full of people who talked fast, laughed loudly, and shouted when they got into political arguments. Ethiopian emigrants. Roaming photographers with shaggy beards and war stories. Doctors and other medical workers with sad, compassionate eyes. Mom would make sure everyone got fed and would sometimes sit and talk intensely with someone in the corner.

She and Mom now moved from the hedge to one of the flower patches. "How glorious this will be in the spring!" Mom said. "We should be planting lily bulbs, and probably dividing these irises. Did you know that the Greek goddess Iris was the personification of the rainbow and she carried messages to the ends of the earth?" She knelt down and started to dig. "My mother's name was Iris, you know. My grandmother, who loved flowers, named her three daughters Iris, Rose, and Lily."

Dakar sat down on the grass. Usually when they were in the mood to talk about families, they talked about Dad's adventuresome one: Dad as a little kid, climbing every step up the 984-foot spire of the Eiffel Tower. Or on the deck of a Dutch liner, seeing the moon over the Atlantic Ocean, or standing at the Acropolis seeing the moon over Athens. Or perched on the shoulders of a spear-shaking warrior in the middle of a big funeral dance. Maybe flowers couldn't compete. "Did she grow petunias like the ones you planted in Maji?" Dakar asked.

Mom made a strange snuffling sound. Was she crying? She rubbed at her right eye, and Dakar saw a streak of dirt there. Dreamily she went on. "My grandmother was born at the turn of the century, and her parents sent her to college at a time when not many women got to go. What do you think she did in college?"

"Got a Ph.D. like Dad?"

"Here," Mom said. "We need to get the tender bulbs like the gladioli out for winter. Dig carefully like this. No, she played basketball. She only weighed eighty-five pounds when she started high school, but she was a quick little guard, or so she said, and her team won all but one game in four years—and they tied that one!"

"I thought women in the olden days sat and embroidered samplers," Dakar said.

"Yes. Well, not Grandma, apparently. She went on playing in college. She once told me that her coach had called her the most natural basketball player he had ever seen. By then she was a running center, and she once told me proudly that she made twenty-eight points in one game. Four boys asked her out that night."

"Is that how she met Grandpa?" Dakar couldn't remember if she had ever felt more contented than sitting here with her hands in the dirt and bulbs, listening to Mom tell family secrets. Mom said Great-Grandma's parents were sure she'd marry one of her classmates, but she fell in love with someone who was wonderful at breaking horses— and hearts. "Nothing that ever happened to my grandma made her lose her spark," Mom added, "and her kids were all adventuresome." Her only son went off to the navy in World War II and died in a prison camp. Rose had a career in radio for a while. "Lily . . ." Mom chuckled. "Well, you're too young to know the old song about the daring young man on the flying trapeze, but Lily actually did fall in love with a trapeze artist when the circus came to town, and she ran off to marry him."

"What about your mom?" Dakar asked.

"I wish you could have known her," Mom said sadly. "She surprised everyone and married a farmer. My dad could find more adventure in a square plot of prairie than most people find in all of Africa. My mother collected *National Geographic* magazines, and we'd study them together. 'I should have joined the circus when I had the chance,' she once hollered at my father."

Dakar remembered the voices from the night before. What did Mom and Dad holler about in the middle of the night? She didn't dare ask.

"Mama adored her sister Lily's visits," Mom said. "So did I. My uncle Otis was a very poetic man, and when he talked, I could imagine what it felt like to soar through the air. His hands felt like the hooves of the lambs I fed every spring—that tough and calloused. One time I asked him if he was ever afraid he would fall. He told me that when the circus was in Los Angeles, by sheer chance he came upon the grave of the Great Cadona, the King of Trapeze. He looked for a long time at the sculpted angel on Cadona's grave. That night, when he heard the *hep* and flew into the catcher's hands, he felt Cadona with him. He came to believe Cadona was living out his own life dreams through him."

Dakar felt an electric excitement squeezing her throat. This had to go in her list of synchronicity.

Mom stood up. "I listened to Uncle Otis's stories, and I promised I would soar. While my friends were trying on lipstick, I was busy dreaming of adventure."

Dakar stood up and stretched her arms. "And you did soar, Mom."

"Yes, I did," Mom said uncertainly. "My poor adventuresome family."

"Why? What happened to them?"

"I'm sure you remember my mother was killed in a plane crash on her way to Maji to see me. My uncle Otis fell from the trapeze bar one night and died. The only one left is your great-aunt Lily, and she's living in my parents' house about five or six hours from here. I don't know why I haven't written to her yet." She started to walk toward the house, her hands full of bulbs. "We should go in. Your dad's almost home."

Dakar nodded. Mom had a weird telepathy about Dad and always seemed to be able to tell when he was near. As Dakar tagged after Mom, she wondered, Did longings pass? She was pretty sure they didn't. They mostly hung around and made people sad, even if you weren't sure why.

When they were finally on their way to the airport, she stared out at the trees. Some of them definitely had yellow streaks. The trees were starting to put on their party clothes for Jakarta.

To make the time pass, she tried to count all the airports she had ever been in, but there were too many. Instead, she'd make a list of words that she especially liked the sounds of: *Jambalaya. Jambo. Simba. Fit-fit. Korra-korro. Buff. Bippy*. She giggled. It took forever to park, even though the airport had only two little parking lots and you could see the main building from both of them. Every minute seemed to stretch out like a long thread unrolling from a spool.

Inside, Dad thumped his hand against his leg nervously. "Can we get Jakarta some Gummi worms?" Dakar asked. "She hasn't had any American candy for a long time."

"Yeah, why not rot her teeth and start her off right?" Dad handed Dakar two dollar bills.

"Will you do it?" she wanted to say. "Please?" What if Gummi worms cost more than two dollars? What was the thing with tax? But she couldn't admit to Dad that she still felt nervous when she had to figure out American money. "*Ayezosh,*" she told herself. "Be brave." Any sixth grader in America knew how to buy Gummi worms.

As she waited in line for the man in front of her

to choose his doughnut, she thought about when she and Mom had sat by the woodstove waiting for Jakarta to come home from boarding school. She remembered the warm smell of Mom's arm, the sleepy excitement of listening for the roar of the Jeep. "Is that it? Is that it?" No, it was always only the roaring of the fire in the stove or the wind roaring in the cedar trees.

Eventually she'd panicked and started to cry. What if the plane didn't land?

She'd somehow been able to sense Mom was as scared as she was. Every week, the mules dutifully climbed the hill behind the house, trotted through Maji town, and then followed the lead horse onto the steep, rough road that led down the mountain to the savanna where Ethiopian Airlines planes landed once a week. The trip was only thirty-two miles, Dad said, but it took two days for the mules to descend 8,000 feet. A few days later, when shouts relayed the news that the mules had managed to trudge back up the mountain, Mom and Dad would rush out—but often they had to sigh over empty mailbags because the plane couldn't land. "Don't cry," Mom had said, crying a little, too. "Oh, I *hope* the plane lands." And then, finally: "Shh, isn't that the Jeep?"

Finally, gloriously, it really was the faint sound

of the Jeep engine. She could remember her night-gown, wet with dew, flapping against her cold legs in the mountain wind as they ran outside. Mom whirled and whirled until her dress twisted around her slender legs. They held hands as the Jeep came around the corner and down the last hill, head-lights shining, seeming to pick up speed on that hill just the way the mules did.

"A dollar fifty," the young woman behind the counter said.

Dakar was startled. She was in North Dakota, not Maji. Planes here didn't circle and circle and then not land because the weather was bad or there were too many animals on the field. They didn't disappear, the hum growing fainter and fainter and finally fading completely away. She handed over the money, relieved that the change was going to be easy.

The woman behind the counter had on an inter-esting turban, and her voice had a lovely accent. She might be from somewhere in Africa. Why would someone like that come to North Dakota? Dakar wondered. Maybe for the university? She wished she weren't too shy to ask.

"Hurry," Dad suddenly called. "People are start-ing to come off. Hey, there she is!"

Dakar raced back. She stared at the people who were trickling down the stairs. "Nah. That's not her."

"It's not," Mom agreed, poking Dad's arm teasingly. "You're so excited you're seeing things."

"Don't be afraid to run up there, just *push* people out of the way," Dakar told herself, bouncing with excitement. "Run up and *fling* your arms around her."

More people came out the door. Then there was a gap when nobody came out. Dakar had been waiting so long she felt paralyzed. Suddenly there Jakarta was. Taller. A little thinner. But most definitely Jakarta. Her eyes flicked over the faces and met Dakar's as Dakar started to run. But Jakarta wasn't leaping down the stairs toward them. She wasn't even walking down. As Dakar pushed her way up the stairs, she saw Jakarta's face crumple like a piece of paper being scrunched up to be thrown away. Then Jakarta burst into tears.

NINE

Dakar was sure she had never been so miserable. She was scrunched in the backseat with one of Jakarta's suitcases digging into her thigh. She wished Jakarta would look at her, but Jakarta was staring out the window.

"Why did you bring me here?" Jakarta sounded as if someone were strangling her.

At least she was finally talking. The whole time they waited for the luggage, all she did was point at her suitcases when they came around on the conveyor belt. "We were worried . . . It isn't safe in Nairobi right now . . . Jakarta, be reasonable." Mom and Dad's words tumbled over one another.

"Then it isn't safe for all my friends who are still there. What about Malika and her family? What about the soccer team? They're all still there."

"I'm sure their parents are there, too," Mom said sharply.

"The bombing didn't have anything to do with us," Jakarta argued. "It's just ethnic tension. Like the fires in the Karura Forest behind our house."

Dakar remembered driving home at dusk and seeing billows of red smoke, streaked with sparks, over the forest. When they got home, she and Jakarta had raced to the balcony off Mom and Dad's bedroom and watched pitchy trees go up with a *whoomp* sound and flashes of flame.

"Some people say the developers started the fire," Jakarta said. "It has something to do with plots that were given away in the forest. I have a Luo friend at school who says, 'When liberation came to Kenya, the Kikuyu did the land grabbing. Now it's our turn.' "

Dad laughed. "Sounds like Kenya politics."

"I want to go back," Jakarta wailed. "And why are there about ten Gummi worms in this big cardboard box? What a waste! It's just like on the airplane when we threw away all those little plastic dishes."

"You can give me the Gummi worms," Dakar muttered, "since they're so wasteful and all."

If Jakarta heard her, she didn't give any sign. "Malika and I made friends with one of the little kids in the Kikuyu village. When he heard I was leaving, he came to the house and gave me a present wrapped in a big leaf. It was one of those plastic dishes from the airplane. That was the most precious thing he could think of to give me. And yesterday we all threw those plastic things in the trash."

"Doesn't she remind you of me?" Dad asked Mom proudly.

Dakar frowned. "Just give her a little room to come back to us," Mom had murmured on the way out to the car. But Dakar didn't *want* to have to give Jakarta room. She knew she was feeling childish, but there it was.

"I remember perfectly when I was a teenager and we visited the States," Dad said. "The Beatles were just getting popular. We got to my cousin's house that first night. Here was this room full of teenagers all waiting to watch the Ed Sullivan program. I had no idea who the Beatles were. I wanted to drop through the floor." After a minute he added, "To this day I have never felt so out of place."

"You'll feel much better once you get over jet lag and have a chance to look around a little bit," Mom told Jakarta.

"Strange," Dad went on. "It's okay to be different in a foreign country but not at home, where it's expected you know it all and that you'll act and dress and talk like your age-group."

"Culture shock," Mom said. "You're feeling culture shock, Jakarta."

Dakar tried to think what had helped when she was feeling culture-shocked. "Want me to show you the high school?" she asked. "They gave us an orientation tour the first day, so I know where things are. Melanie's cousin goes there, so we could ask him questions."

"Who's Melanie?"

Dakar bit her thumbnail. Be careful what you tell her. Was Jakarta ready to hear that it was perfectly fine to have friends here?

"We should stop at the high school right now," Mom said. "I'm sure Jakarta would like to see it."

"I wouldn't like to see it," Jakarta said. "Not at all."

But Dad pulled into a space in front of the school, anyway. "Great idea. Let's get you registered," he said. "Then you can just go home and sleep without worrying."

Luckily for everyone, Dakar thought, they must have gotten there in the middle of a period. No one was in the halls. In the office Jakarta hummed under her breath the whole time, as if Mom and Dad were registering some other daughter. When the secretary handed over a locker combination, she spoke for the first time since getting to the school. "Will you help me find my locker?" she whispered to Dakar.

Dakar wondered if Jakarta would look into any of the rooms as they walked by, but she didn't. A boy with a white cane walked down the hall toward them, swinging the cane fiercely in front of him, looking like the grim reaper. Otherwise, they didn't see anyone.

Suddenly Jakarta grabbed Dakar's arm. "Is there going to be anyone here who looks like me?"

Dakar looked at her in surprise. "Sure," she said quickly. Then she tried to figure out what Jakarta meant. Had she ever seen anyone who looked like Jakarta? No. Jakarta was *distinctive*. That was one thing that made her so great.

In Maji, Jakarta used to ask Mom to tell her birth story over and over. "Your grandfather was African American," Mom would say. "Your grandmother was Japanese. They fell in love because of World War Two, but those times were a different day and time, and those World War Two babies were rejected by the families on both sides. Your dad ended up being adopted by an American couple. He grew up to be an amazing young man— talented, funny, the kind who seems to charm everyone instantly—and when he decided to go traveling around Asia to rediscover his roots, he certainly charmed your mother, who was the

French teacher's aide at the school where I was teaching in Indonesia."

"So my mother was French?" Jakarta would say every time.

"No, she was Iranian, and she was very young. It was her first time away from home. When she got pregnant with you, she had no idea what to do. Then, when your father was suddenly killed in a car accident, she cried every day for a month and told me over and over that her parents would never help her out with the baby. I was worried sick."

"And you took her under your wing," Jakarta loved to say, taking a deep breath.

"Your father and I both did. We held your mother's hands the night you were born. A few days later she wrote you the most loving, tender letter that she asked me to put away until you were eighteen. Her age. Then she put you in our arms and went home to her own mother."

Jakarta would let out the breath she'd been holding, and Mom would finish by saying, "You were born surrounded by love, Jakarta. I had the oddest sensation that your genetic father was there in the room, too. One time, when we all were lying on the white sands of Sanur Beach, he cupped his hands into an instrument and played songs for us.

The night you were born, I would swear I heard that haunting whistle of a song as I stared down at your tiny face."

Too bad Jakarta wasn't tiny anymore, because she was suddenly trying to squeeze inside her locker. "Hey. Close the door," Jakarta said. "I need to see if it's big enough so I can hide in here if I need to."

"Your head won't go in," Dakar argued. "You're too tall."

Jakarta squeezed back out, fiddled with the combination, and finally said, "Smooth as gravy." As they walked back, she asked, "Think I should get my spear out of the footlocker and bring it to school?"

"I don't think so." Dakar tried to see Jakarta's face. "The worst thing they do in middle school is just dump your books. You carry them on your side. If you stick them out in front, they can run by and dump them." She decided not to tell Jakarta what Melanie's cousin had said about ninth graders spitting in the salad dressing. "Come see this." She dragged Jakarta over. "Wall o' jocks," she said triumphantly.

Jakarta laughed, and Dakar felt a warm sweetness oozing in her throat. "I got the idea from you," she said shyly. "Because you made up the wall o' burghers in Amsterdam. Remember?" A girl rushed by them without a glance. Dakar studied her as she walked away and then looked Jakarta over. "Maybe we should go shopping after this."

"Why? I'm not going to pay seventy dollars or something for some pair of jeans."

"You wouldn't be paying," Dakar said. "Mom and Dad would."

Jakarta just shrugged. Dakar thought about the clothes in Melanie's catalog. What would Jakarta say about them if she thought seventy dollars for jeans was bad?

"Are you tired?" Dad said when they were back in the car. "I'm sure you'll feel better once you get over your jet lag."

"Why don't you take a nap?" Mom said.

"I'm not tired," Jakarta said. After a minute she let out a kind of muffled moan. "Actually, I think I'm sick. Really sick."

Jakarta was in bed the rest of the week. "How is she?" Melanie asked every day.

Dakar always said something like "She'll be fine. Getting better every day." But it was hard. When Jakarta was well enough to get up for dinner and Mom said, "Isn't the corn tender and sweet here?" Jakarta said that she preferred the chewy field corn they used to roast over the fire. When Dad asked if Jakarta had taken all her doses of medicine, Jakarta mumbled that she'd just as soon die as have to live here.

Dakar felt sick herself, trudging to school every day, watching one small stand of trees across from the house turning color early. What if Jakarta insisted on going back as soon as she got well? Why did Mom and Dad seem so impatient with each other? She lit a candle and waited for the universe to give her some idea about what she could do. But no ideas came.

Sunday evening Jakarta said, "I reeeeally need to jog."

"Great!" Mom's voice was frizzy with tension and relief at the same time. "I'll go with you."

Maybe it was going to be okay, Dakar thought as she sat on the porch and watched Mom and Jakarta start off. She took off her shoes and wiggled her toes against the warm steps, then leaned back on her elbows. Clouds had filled up most of the sky, but a little smudge of blue was still above their house letting sunshine spill through right onto their porch. Sunshine was always a good sign.

She tried to remember what it had been like for

her the first day. The house had seemed big and strange. Cottonwood had seemed little and tidy. She'd been homesick for everything, especially Maji, even though she hadn't lived there for years. But now she liked the big trees in the yard here and the way the ceiling sloped down in her room.

After a while she saw them coming back, far down the block. Jakarta sprinted toward her, arms pumping, hair flying all over, Donbirra graceful. "Abebe Bikila," Jakarta shouted, lifting her arms in a victory salute.

"Who's that?"

"First guy in history to win the Olympic marathon twice—way before our time. For stamina, it's great to train in a high altitude like Ethiopia." She sagged to the step beside Dakar. "Usually I do sprints—because of soccer. A long run feels like a treat."

It took a while longer for Mom to stagger up. She grabbed the porch railing and pulled herself up, hand over hand, laughing and panting at the same time. "You've gotten too fast for me," she said, collapsing beside Jakarta.

They sat without saying anything. Dakar could hear Mom still breathing hard, but not Jakarta. Jakarta's face was barely pink, and her breathing sounded even and sure. Their patch of sunshine was gone, and a light wind had blown up, but in the one stand of birch trees the treetops were like match tips, blazing yellow gold. "I'm going to sit here forever," Dakar said.

"Why forever?" Mom asked.

"I don't know. It's a nice even number."

Inside, the phone rang. "Dad'll get it," Dakar said. She didn't want anyone to move. She wanted to reach out and put her arms around both of them. She could always say the wind was making her cold.

"Deborah?" Dad called.

"Coming." Mom got up.

"Don't go," Dakar wanted to say, but she didn't. She listened to the door sigh shut behind Mom.

After a few minutes Jakarta asked, "Has Mom been okay here?"

"She's been fine," Dakar said. "Sometimes she's been really happy, in fact."

"Did you guys visit her hometown?"

Dakar shook her head.

"Why not?"

"Well, it's a long drive, you know. We were getting settled. After that, Dad needed to spend three weeks in Minneapolis. Then school started. And maybe she was afraid to go by herself."

"Afraid of what? The driving?"

"Yeah, I guess." Dakar ran her finger along the rough porch floor. "The driving." She didn't want to say the rest. Maybe afraid the North Dakota part of her heart had been frozen so long it couldn't thaw. Maybe afraid that if it did thaw, the ice would leave big holes for hoodies to crawl through. "After the bombing I was afraid that—" The door opened. Dakar stopped, assuming it was Mom coming back. But it was Dad.

"Mom's aunt Lily was in a car accident," Dad said. "She's going to be fine, but they think she has a broken leg."

"Who's Aunt Lily?" Jakarta asked.

"Grandma's sister. Your mom's going to go and help out."

"That's lousy," Jakarta said. "That's really lousy." She scrambled up, pushed past Dad, and disappeared inside.

Dad gave a frustrated shrug. "Everything is going to be fine," he said to Dakar. Then he disappeared, too.

Dakar sat on the porch and watched as the rain started. Soon a drizzle like the long, slow ripple of a jazz song was soaking the trees, putting out the matches one by one.

FROM DAKAR'S BOOK
OF LISTS AND THOUGHTS

At Mombasa we were supposed to have such a glorious vacation. But when we went snorkeling, I panicked every time I had to put my face in the water. And while they were looking at coral gardens under the sea, I got two sea urchin prongs in my foot and also split my toe. So I spent the rest of the time limping around our hotel room.

I used to think it was just me. But now I can't remember if Mom had a glorious time or not.

◆ ◇ ◆ ◇ ◆ ◇ ◆ ◇ ◆ ◇ ◆ ◇ ◆ ◇ ◆ ◇ ◆ ◇ ◆ ◇ ◆ ◇ ◆ ◇ ◆ ◇ ◆ ◇ ◆ ◇

TEN

◆ ◇ ◆ ◇ ◆ ◇ ◆ ◇ ◆ ◇ ◆ ◇ ◆ ◇ ◆ ◇ ◆ ◇ ◆ ◇ ◆ ◇ ◆ ◇ ◆ ◇ ◆ ◇

The next morning it was still raining. Dakar dreamed that she had just told a story and the audience was applauding politely. She woke to the sound of the rain against the windowpane. The gentle clapping made her remember the little rains on a tin roof. A clattering of angry voices down the hall was more like the big rains on tin. She lay stiff and still, trying to hear the words. Wisps eked through. Jakarta was arguing with Dad about school. But they *never* argued with Dad.

The argument was still going on when Dakar went down to eat breakfast. "Mom's leaving tomorrow," Jakarta was saying to Dad. "I need to spend a day with her. I need her to take me shopping."

Dakar shot a look at Jakarta, but Jakarta stared down at her bowl.

"All right," Dad finally said with exasperation. "But this is the only day you're going to miss. The sooner you get to school, the sooner you're going to make new friends and stop feeling so out of place."

"The sooner the wildebeests will stomp me," Jakarta muttered.

Dakar pushed away from the table and went back upstairs.

Mom was dressed and lying on top of the covers. She patted the side of the bed. "Off to school?"

"Yeah." The bed squeaked as Dakar settled onto it. She reached out and stroked Mom's arm.

"Got an umbrella?"

"I think it stopped raining while I was eating breakfast."

"It isn't quite the way we thought it would be, is it?" Mom said.

"Not at all." Dakar blinked and bit her thumb. "Why isn't it?"

"Just those famous teenage mood swings, I guess."

Mom murmured something else, but her voice was so soft that Dakar couldn't hear. A burst of shouting drifted up from downstairs. "I've never heard either Jakarta or Dad be this way before," Dakar said.

"Your father hasn't spent much time in the same house as a teenage Jakarta before, either." Mom pulled Dakar down for a kiss. "Okay, I don't like it, either. But it's nothing to worry about. You have a good day in school, all right?"

As she left the house, Dakar tried to figure out why people were always telling her not to worry. There was plenty to worry about. When she got close to Melanie's house, she hesitated, but for some reason she didn't feel like stopping. Everything was such a jumble. "How's Jakarta?" Melanie would say again in her bright, eager voice. And what was Dakar going to say? She rushed on to school, not even stopping at her locker before she headed down the stairs.

"That poor child," the cook said, shaking her head, when Dakar poured out the story. "That poor little lost child." She clicked her tongue.

Dakar watched the cook's fingers pressing pizza dough into a tray. "What about me?" she said. "Why isn't anyone worrying about me?"

"Oh, yes," the cook said. "You're a poor child, too. Too bad we've got to take the bitter with the sweet, Africa child. Did they tell you that in Africa?"

Like pomegranates. "I just don't think things should be bitter all the time."

"Oh, my," the cook said. "Life can be a dry and weary land where no water is. But I don't b'lieve things are bitter all the time."

The kitchen was warm with the thick, yeasty smell of dough rising. "Here's one thing I will tell you," the cook said. "You tell her to go to school—"

"Because she has to grab on to her education," Dakar said.

"Because she has to grab on to her education. And you tell her to watch out for my son, Pharo, when she gets to school."

Dakar was surprised. "You have a kid who goes to high school?"

The cook chuckled.

"You have a son named Pharaoh? Why didn't you give him a better name than that?"

The cook scooped tomato paste out of a can with her fingers. "When that boy was born, I called him Moses, but my husband never could tolerate that name. He said, 'If he's Moses, he's in charge of freeing other people. But who's ever going to free this boy from the bondage?' My husband had come to study at the university, but now he was homesick and tired of people's attitudes. So we pushed and pulled that poor baby's name back and forth, back and forth. I called him Moses. My husband took to calling him Pharo, just to make me mad, I b'lieve."

Dakar tried to imagine the cook sitting in a living room in this picket fence town, arguing with her husband.

"Well, the homesickness weighed on my hus-

band and weighed on him. Finally he just quit
school. He went back home. My heart was like wax
then. It was melted within my breast. But all I said
was, 'Good. I can call my boy Moses without any
complaints now.'"

"Why didn't you go, too?" Dakar asked.

The cook slid the pizza on a pan. "Well, there
was my vow not to put this body onto an airplane
again. More so, I wanted my boy to grow up in a
place where he could grab hold of an education.
Still, I did fret. Finally, I opened my Bible and put
my finger on the page to see if God would send me
a message directly."

Dakar nodded. She knew people who did that. A
girl in Egypt said her grandfather used to do the
same thing with the Koran.

"My finger fell on 'God is the anchor of my soul.'
That's a message, I said. My body is meant to stay
put and not go flopping all around the world."

Dakar shook her head dubiously. "I don't know.
The Bible says God is light, too. Light flickers all
around."

"It doesn't go leaping from the candle," the cook
said. "So we stayed put. But we started getting the
letters. It was always Pharo this and Pharo that.
And one day when I called my little boy Moses, he

said, 'My name is Pharo.' And I thought, well, let him have what's left from his daddy."

The bell rang. The cook pointed one doughy finger at the door.

"Okay," Dakar said. "I'm going. And I'll tell Jakarta."

Having something to tell Jakarta helped the day go faster. In math class Melanie tossed a note over when the teacher wasn't looking. "Where were you?" it said. "My cousin says everyone is *très* curious about Jakarta."

Dakar had never passed a note in class before. "Sorry," she scribbled. "Come over for supper. My mom won't care. At least *you* can meet Jakarta." Her face itched as she waited for the right moment to toss the note back. Dakar, the former Good Kid, the former Follower, was now also a note tosser.

When they opened the door of the house, a hot, peppery smell rushed out—a smell of Maji. Dakar gave a luxurious sigh, feeling like a little kid.

"What is it?" Melanie asked. "What's that smell?"

"Come on," Dakar said, heading for the kitchen. "You'll see."

Mom looked up and swiped at her sweaty face.

"You're Melanie," she said. "I'm so glad you're here. We need lots and lots of onions chopped. Both of you can help."

She looked great, Dakar thought with a *clunk* of relief, handing a knife to Melanie and grabbing one for herself. "How did you manage Maji food?"

"Jakarta smuggled the injera and the bere bere pepper out for a surprise. We're making the wat."

"What wat?" Melanie laughed and sliced through the onion with an awkward chop.

Dakar made a face. "I've only heard that joke about fifty thousand times, you know."

"Dakar," Mom said, "I need to tell you—"

The door slammed. Suddenly Jakarta was there, all lighted up like a pumpkin. "Heaven," she said. "I'm in heaven. I love it, love it, love it. Hey." She grabbed the knife out of Melanie's hand. "What are you doing? You're chopping those onions waaaaay too thick."

"This is Melanie," Dakar said hastily. Good. That was over. "Come on," she said to Melanie. "Let her do it since she's so thrilled to. The onions are making me cry, anyway."

"Wow," Melanie whispered as they left the kitchen. "*Très* intimidating."

Dakar nodded. Behind them, Mom and Jakarta

were talking in Amharic and laughing. She thought about taking Melanie up to her room, but there were too many private things like the gourd Wondemu gave her the day she left Maji and—even worse—the clock that blinked constantly because Dakar didn't know how to set the time. She took her downstairs, instead, and showed her the room in the basement. "Just like a horsetail," Melanie said, picking up a fly whisk and whisking herself with it.

"That's the point."

When they came back up, Dad was laughing uproariously as Jakarta tried to show him how to do the *eskista* dance, shaking her shoulders skillfully, one at a time and then together. "Your dad's a riot," Melanie whispered.

Dad and Jakarta were still in a boisterous mood at supper, scooping up big mouthfuls of wat with the injera and feeding each other the way people did at feasts. Dakar watched them contentedly, her mouth exploding with the peppery and sour tastes she loved. Why couldn't things always be festive like this?

"How's the girls' soccer team here?" Jakarta asked between bites.

Melanie swished a piece of injera around her plate and nibbled the edge of it. "Uh . . ." she said.

"I don't think there's a girls' soccer team," Dakar said quickly.

"Nope," Melanie said. "No boys' soccer team even."

Jakarta raised one eyebrow. "Whose idea was it to live here?"

Mom looked a bit defensive. "When I saw the pictures of this house, it seemed just right for what I had in mind. We could also afford it, and it's a manageable distance from the other things we need."

Jakarta frowned.

"Come on," Mom said. "There must be something you like about being in the United States. We can drive at night and not be afraid."

Dad smiled his most bedazzling smile—as if he were sun, Dakar thought, and they were planets orbiting around him. "I never worried about driving at night," he said.

"Living here has to be better than some things we've tried," Mom told Jakarta. "Boarding school, for example."

"You know," Dad said, "I never realized that Dakar had trouble sleeping in school. I wonder why no one ever told us."

Dakar kicked at the table leg. Did Dad have to talk about something embarrassing like that in front of Melanie? She concentrated on making her eyes cool and smooth as eggshells. She was Donbirra. Nobody needed to know what she was thinking.

"It's all fine to say now why didn't anybody tell us," Jakarta said, suddenly fierce. "You didn't know because you didn't want to know. Because if you knew, how could you have chosen your precious work over us?"

Dakar was shocked. She didn't know where to look. Not at Mom's stunned face. Not at Dad, either. A Sahara of silence stretched out until she thought she would have to say something.

But Jakarta was the one who broke the silence. "I'm leaving." She got up from the table and ran for the front door.

"Wait." Dakar pushed her chair away.

Behind her, she heard Melanie say, "Wait, wait."

They must look funny, she thought. Jakarta running down the sidewalk, Dakar running after. And she could hear Melanie's footsteps behind her. Luckily, Jakarta slowed up and let them catch up.

"Shall we show you around?" Dakar asked. "There's this great place."

"Sure." Jakarta stared into the distance, her voice trembling. "Show me around, okay?"

"Jakarta isn't anything like what you said," Melanie whispered as they walked. "Not anything at all."

Dakar signaled for her to be quiet. "Thanks for helping with supper."

"How do you get the onion into such little pieces?" Melanie asked Jakarta. "You know, I never actually touched an onion before."

Jakarta whirled around. "How did you become friends with this nimrod?" she asked Dakar. She marched ahead of them a few steps.

"What's a nimrod?" Melanie whispered.

"Nimrod was a mighty hunter in the Bible," Dakar whispered back. Calling someone a nimrod made a good boarding school insult. It sounded bad, but you could always say, innocently, "I was comparing you to a mighty hunter." She shook her head. How could anyone possibly be in sixth grade and not have touched an onion?

"Let's take Jakarta to the magic place," Melanie said cheerfully.

Dakar hesitated. But why not? Usually it was Jakarta who discovered all the cool places—the bat cave behind the waterfall, with its musty smell. The maze of paths wild pigs had trampled out.

Jakarta turned around to look at them and

waved her arm in a big arc. "I guess some of the leaves are pretty, but why would anyone live here when you could have fuchsia and orange bougainvillea and roses and lilies and carnations and pink pyrethrum?"

"Wait until you see the best place," Melanie said. "Dakar said it's the kind of place where you could fight the Allalonestone."

Dakar tried to swallow, but a lump of ice was caught in her throat.

Jakarta turned and looked at Dakar. "You told her about the Allalonestone?"

If she weren't already turning to ice, Dakar thought, Jakarta's voice would do it. Liver. Stomach. She couldn't even feel her fingers anymore. She opened her mouth. Shut it. Fish mouth. She wanted to say no, but that would be pretty pointless.

"It's okay," Melanie said cheerfully. "I know the incantation."

Jakarta looked at Dakar. "Don't . . . say . . . a . . . word," she said. "I'm going for a walk. A long, long walk." She started to run.

"You don't know your way around this town," Dakar yelled after her. Jakarta didn't even hesitate. "She doesn't know where she's going," Dakar said to Melanie when even the sound of Jakarta's footsteps had died away. "She'll get lost and never come home, and it will be all your fault." She knew she was being irrational.

Melanie looked stricken. "Someone will show her the way home."

"I said not to tell *anyone*," Dakar said.

"But I just said it to Jakarta," Melanie said. "She helped make the incantation up." Her eyes were like a scared ferret's eyes, Dakar thought. For some reason those small, scared eyes just made Dakar all the angrier.

"You promised," Dakar said. "You gave me your total, solemn oath. You're not a true friend. You're not my friend at all. Stay completely *away* from me from now on."

She ran all the way home, hoping Mom or Dad would know what to do. When she opened the door, the smell of bere bere was the only thing left of the supper. She couldn't even hear any voices. "Dakar, relax," she told herself. People didn't vanish. "Mom?" she called. "Dad?"

The note was on the table. "Gone to take your mom to rent a car," it said in Dad's handwriting. "I love you both." That was Mom's writing. "Be good. I'll be back soon." After that. Mom had scribbled in little, shaky letters, "Jakarta, don't you dare think for a minute that I didn't agonize even more than you did over boarding school."

Dakar grabbed the note and tore it into bits. "I hate Jakarta," she said out loud in the empty room. "I wish she had never come home." Now she was truly and totally ice.

ELEVEN

When you were ice, Dakar discovered, you didn't have to think. Or maybe that wasn't right. You still had think so you could fig- ure out things like integers, but you didn't have to feel anything. And you didn't have to think about feelings.

When she saw Jakarta getting ready to go off to her first morning of school, she knew instantly that it wasn't very smart for Jakarta to wear a *khanga* or carry a *kiondo* slung over her shoulder, but she didn't have to care—and she didn't care.

Jakarta argued in the kitchen with Dad about it. "Why not?" Dakar heard Jakarta shout. "I don't mind what wildebeests think. Why should you mind?" But Dakar didn't care that they were argu- ing again. She was ice.

When you were ice, you didn't have to worry about walking with Jakarta to school but could watch her stride off, watch her leg muscles ripple under her skirt. You could drag your own slow way and walk by the high school door as if Jakarta were someone else's sister. Jakarta was standing off a little to the side. Kids were eyeing her, but no one had gotten very close, and Dakar didn't blame them. Jakarta had a murderous look in her eyes, and Dakar half expected her to start swinging her *kiondo*. Pow. Pow. Dakar imagined kids falling right and left, holding their heads. But Jakarta didn't start swinging. She just looked around and said loudly, "Yes, I grew up in Africa, and no, I never saw Tarzan. So don't anyone bother to ask."

When you were ice, you didn't have to shiver inside, praying that a savior would show up for Jakarta. Actually, though, a savior did arrive. He was taller than she was, and he walked right through the crowd of kids and looked at Jakarta. "Hey."

"Hey," she said back in a fierce voice.

"My mom told me to look for you. I'm Pharo." Jakarta looked at him for a minute. Then the two of them went off.

"Whoa," Dakar heard someone say. "That girl is Tarzan all right." But that was okay. She was ice. She didn't have to feel anything.

When you were ice, you could sit in math class and watch Melanie giggling with another girl and you didn't even have to wonder what they were writing about in that note they were tossing back and forth when Mr. Johnson's back was turned. You didn't even make the effort to see the cook. You found a corner of the cafeteria and ate as fast as you could.

You didn't have to feel anything after school, either, when the telephone rang and it was Mom saying, "I'm sorry I had to leave so suddenly. Dakar? Dakar, are you there? I tried to tell you when we were chopping the onions that I talked to Aunt Lily's doctor, and he said I should get here as quickly as possible." You didn't have to feel. You could just say, "Uh-huh," and get off the phone.

That night, when Jakarta and Dad sat at the table having a hot political argument, you could tell yourself it was nothing; you were used to political discussions. You could pretend you didn't notice that Jakarta and Dad seemed to have grown rough edges and rubbed against each other like a cheese grater rubbing against a cheese grater.

The next night, when Jakarta and Dad sat in stone silence, you could be a stone, too. It was safe being a stony lump of ice. You didn't even have to ache with longing to hear Mom's voice.

Jakarta must have been aching, too. "I want to call Mom," she told Dad late that week. "Please show me how to make a long-distance call."

"You can't," he said gently. "Aunt Lily doesn't have a phone on the farm. Apparently she likes life reeeeal simple. But Mom said she would call us from a neighbor's house every week."

"Why did you make her go?" Jakarta asked ferociously. When Dad started to answer, she put her hands over her ears and ran out the door.

After Dakar helped Dad do the dishes, she went out and found Jakarta sitting on the porch. Jakarta had slipped her arms out of her sweater, wrapping the knitted arms around herself in a kind of hug. She'd been crying again, and the tears left shiny streaks on her face.

For the first time since Mom left, Dakar felt a pang. Uh-oh. This pain didn't feel good. Was the ice melting?

"What kinds of trees are those?" Jakarta asked, pointing.

Dakar sat down. She'd stood under those very trees her first week, feeling confused and lost while bits of white fluff floated down, covering her shoulders. She'd been wondering if the white stuff could possibly be snow, although she was pretty sure the air had to be colder to make snow.

A girl with purple hair had ridden up on a bike and slowed down to stare.

"What *is* this stuff?" Dakar asked.

"Kid-hey. Why do you think they call it a cottonwood tree?"

"I didn't know they did."

"For weird. I guess you're not from around here."

Dakar winced, remembering. She sometimes saw the girl with purple hair in the cafeteria and walked as far away from her as possible. Why was she feeling twinges that could make her wince? The ice floes must be breaking up. Fretfully she pointed to and named the ones she'd learned: birch, cottonwood, Norwegian maple, oak.

"I miss *our* trees," Jakarta said.

Dakar nodded. "The frangipani tree. And jacaranda."

"Thirty-foot-tall ficus trees with fat, shiny leaves," Jakarta said. "Rubber trees. Pepper trees, bottlebrush trees, mango, avocado, hibiscus."

"Don't worry," Dakar said suddenly. "Mom will come back soon."

Jakarta shook her head. "I don't think so. By the way, sweet one, I'm sorry I got so mad about the incantation and all." She wriggled the sweater up and stretched out her hand.

Dakar let Jakarta pull her close and then leaned her head against Jakarta's shoulder. She was definitely feeling things again; something was wringing and twisting her stomach like a washcloth. "I didn't think it was that big a deal," she whispered.

"Do you even remember what pulled Mom inside the Allalonestone that time?" Jakarta asked.

"Of course," Dakar said. "Her mom was killed in a plane crash on her way to visit us in Maji."

"Partly," Jakarta said. "But that was the second death. Remember the first one? I guess you wouldn't. I guess it would be like asking if I remember anything about Indonesia."

Dakar stiffened. Was that pain what it felt like when a liver thawed? Jakarta stroked her forehead the way Melanie might rub Gingerpuff. "We had a brother," Jakarta said suddenly. "You don't remember him at all?"

Dakar pulled back, trying to see Jakarta's face in the glow of the streetlamp.

"He was born right after we got to Ethiopia," Jakarta said. "He was only about four months old when we moved to Maji. One night Mom got up to check on him and he was . . . just . . . dead. They never did know why."

Dakar squeezed her eyes shut, trying to remember. Was even a scrap of memory stored way back there? She thought she could catch a splinter of Mom crying. "Why didn't anyone tell me?"

"Mom never wanted anyone to talk about him, and she got frantic if anybody tried. Dad and the yard workers dug a grave. You walked around telling everyone, 'Our baby has gone to heaven. Our baby has gone to heaven.' Mom planted flowers all over the grave. She always cried if she saw us playing near it, so I told you an evil enchantress had put a spell on it and we couldn't go near it."

Dakar nodded, remembering.

"A year later Dad was away on a trip, and the runners brought her the news of the airplane crash. The crash happened on the very same day our brother had died. At first Mom thought they were talking about Dad. Then she realized it was her mother. She went in her room and didn't come out."

"I completely remember that," Dakar said.

"I was *terrified*," Jakarta said. "I was, what, eight years old? Nine? I made up all those things just to keep you doing something. The schoolboys kept fixing meals for us, so I knew we wouldn't starve."

"We went on a quest," Dakar said. "You told me all about the hoodies and the Allalonestone. I believed you."

Jakarta laughed. "It was weird that she came out on the exact day I made up the incantation."

"And Dad showed up that night, and it was all over."

"It was all over," Jakarta repeated. "But I don't think it was all over for Mom. I think she's been waiting a long, long time to mourn everything. And there's another reason why she's not coming back. Because when she does, Dad will make a stink until we leave here, and she doesn't want to leave."

Thursday morning when Jakarta and Dakar walked to school, Melanie hurried out of her own house and walked behind them, about half a block back. Every time Dakar turned around, Melanie was looking at her with hopeful eyes. Dakar didn't say anything, but she felt a secret flush of joy.

That evening she and Dad and Jakarta sat on the front porch cracking walnuts, laughing, telling stories of camping trips. "Remember German Wuha?" Jakarta asked.

Dakar nodded, dreamy, and leaned her head against Dad's arm. The river at German Wuha was wide and warm, and she felt safe and thrilled all at the same time as they rippled down it on their air mattresses. Mom stood in the river laughing and whisking water at them, water that dried instantly on her shoulders in the hot sun.

"I took off swimming one afternoon," Dad said. "I was having quite a workout when suddenly I rounded a bend and came face-to-face with a wild buffalo." Dakar could hear his laugh rumbling in his chest. "African buffalo may not look like much, but they can be extremely dangerous. They're a good match for any lion."

"Did you know that hippos kill more human beings every year in Africa than any other large mammal?" Jakarta asked. "It's the animals you wouldn't expect that are really scary, isn't it?"

Dakar swallowed. "What did you do?" The elephant was starting toward her, shuddering the ground. "Take a step back," Dad was saying quietly, urgently. No, this was a different story, a different time. And no trackers with guns. Just Dad, alone in the river.

He laughed again. "Turned around and churned out of there as fast as I could go."

Later that night, Mom called. "What are you doing?" Dakar asked when it was her turn to talk. She could hear Jakarta's breathing on the extension.

"I can't believe how many people around here remember me." Mom's voice sounded young. "Everyone talks to me about my parents. I walk out to the graveyard every day and sit by their graves. Does that sound morbid? Oh, Aunt Lily is getting a little bit better, too."

By the time they got off the phone, Jakarta and Dad were arguing with each other again. Dakar didn't get it. She'd seen Dad swap stories with Kenyan businessmen, Ethiopian ambassadors with aristocratic faces, nearly naked nomads who drank the blood and milk of their cows for supper. But he couldn't seem to connect with Jakarta. He'd ask her things like "Why are you pushing your food around your plate? What are you eating at school these days?"

"Food," Jakarta would say. "Or homework once in a while. But only when I need to." If Dad tried to give her advice, she'd say, "I have two words for you. Puh. Shaw."

When Dad asked Jakarta how her classes were going, she admitted, "Not as appalling as I thought. The science curriculum is actually pretty interesting. Did you know botanists recently found the biggest living thing ever discovered? It's a tree-killing fungus that started from a microscopic spore and has been spreading rhizomorphs for about 2,400 years."

Dad looked at her with a triumphant expression, but when he opened his mouth, she said quickly, "My English teacher, on the other hand, talks so slowly that you can dream a whole daydream in between each of her words."

Over the weekend Jakarta and Dakar sat in the living room doing homework and swapping memories. "Do you remember," Jakarta said, "how we made partners for the frogs when the king of the water babies decided to give a ball?"

"No," Dakar said. And then: "Yes! Oh, I do remember." They both started to laugh and talk at the same time. At first Dakar had been afraid of the calla lilies that looked like gloating mouths with long yellow tongues. But then Jakarta had pulled the pale yellow stamens from the calla lilies and showed Dakar how to dress them in Mom's petunias. Nothing would ever be as beautiful as the calla lily princesses in their ruffles and ruffles of red, purple, and pink petunia dresses. The brightest petunias were in the enchanted garden, but they'd dared go there only once. How odd to think that she had a baby brother buried in Maji. "Do you remember him?" she asked Jakarta.

"No, not really. He wrapped his hand around my wrist. His hair was kind of reddish like yours." She hesitated. "Let's talk about something that isn't so sad, okay?"

" 'Tusker,' " Dakar said in the low, dramatic voice of the ad. " 'Tusker . . . my country. My beer.' "

" 'Don't say bread,' " Jakarta sang.

" 'Say supaloaf,' " Dakar finished. They giggled, tossing memories back and forth like socks.

"Remember the teeth in the road in Nairobi that would bite your car tires?"

"And how weird it felt at first to drive on the left?"

"And going to Amsterdam for vacation?"

"Remember the Rijksmuseum, where we ditched Mom and Dad and spent the day with just the two of us? It was raining."

Dakar grinned. They'd stopped in front of anything bizarre or gory. "Remember that headless guy in the painting? Remember that in India a raised big toe is a sign of vigor?"

"Remember when you ordered *parmaham* thinking it was Parmesan cheese and it was ham?"

"Remember making up fake Dutch? Remember *der schteppen yen?*" Remember? Remember?

"I want to tell the same stories over and over," Jakarta said later that evening as she brushed out her hair.

The air was strangely warm. Dad said this was Indian summer. "Why the same ones?" Dakar asked. "Can I do your hair?"

Jakarta handed the brush to Dakar. Her hair was wavy and black, and Dakar loved the way it felt. Jakarta had always brushed Dakar's hair in boarding school. Now she felt good to be taking care of Jakarta. "There's no way I'm going to forget it all," Jakarta said in a low voice, tipping her head back. "Telling the details, over and over . . . that's the only way I know to keep Africa from disappearing forever."

It was going to be okay, Dakar thought as she brushed. Jakarta was settling. She herself was perfectly happy to be back to being Jakarta's shadow.

She hardly noticed when Melanie didn't come out of her house to follow them Monday morning. Next time Dakar saw her, she was walking with the purple-haired girl in the hall. It was a shock, but Dakar reminded herself that everything was going to be fine. Jakarta was back to take care of her again. If she was careful not to be a wart, maybe pretty soon Jakarta and Dad would even get more used to each other and go back to being the laughing, adventuring pair they had always been, and the three of them would have lots of fun. And maybe Mom would reconnect with her roots and then come home.

That was before basketball changed everything.

TWELVE

It started, as all the other trouble seemed to start these days, at the dinner table. Jakarta said, "Pharo and I were watching old videotapes of Timberwolves games. The Timberwolves make a lot of the other NBA teams look like stodgy old men."

Dad stared at her without his usual interested, amused expression. Maybe Jakarta had hit a nerve. Not that he was stodgy. Or old. "I actually can't think of anything more stupid," Dad said, "than a bunch of grown men running around a court chasing a little ball. The time and money that go into sports in this country are obscene."

Dakar waggled her eyebrows at Jakarta. Not a bad time to quit?

The old Jakarta would have quit or made a joke. "I saw Garnett make a great basket today." Jakarta faked a basket in the air. "Maybe if you had seen it, you'd change your mind. They're so much fun to watch. Vivid. Elegant. Edgy."

"What a waste." Dad waved one arm, but it was a helpless gesture.

Dakar had seen the look on his face before. When Dad couldn't bear injustice or stupidity or the pain of the world being so totally different from the way he just *knew* it should be, he would get a baffled, wounded-elephant look in his eyes. "Watch out," Dakar wanted to say. Wounded elephants could charge, and pain made them not care who got hurt. But Jakarta didn't stop.

"All cultures have games," Jakarta said. "In Ethiopia and Kenya people sometimes kill each other over them, right? How's that for taking games seriously? You always said the most important thing is to pay attention, not try to make people over in our own image."

"How was the library today?" Dakar asked Dad. Her skin felt too tight for her face.

Dad shook his fork at Jakarta, punctuating his words. "People here distract themselves with games," he said. "They use games to avoid looking at the hard things that matter most. How futile to choose to spend your life throwing a ball through a hoop."

"You always said *love* can't just be a word." Jakarta was pushing back her chair as she talked. She stood and leaned toward Dad, both hands on the table. "You said you have to be willing to live with people and listen to them and share their lives wherever they are. Well, maybe I want to share basketball players' lives. Where they are." She spit out the last three words as if they tasted like mud.

"I don't think . . ." Dad said.

But by now Jakarta was nearly out the door. Dad pushed his chair away, too, and headed upstairs. Dakar looked around at the table. It wasn't even her turn to do the dishes.

The next morning, when she banged on Jakarta's door, Jakarta yelled, "Go without me." So Dakar did, feeling hurt and confused. Maybe it was because of the confusion that when she saw Melanie come out of her house, she slowed down and let Melanie catch up. "I thought North Dakota was supposed to be cold," she said as Melanie ran up, panting and grinning.

"It will be," Melanie said. "Pretty soon we'll probably be wearing Russells to school every day. Don't worry, though. We'll show you everything. I'm sure you were never cold in Africa."

Dakar scowled. Someone she thought could be a true friend didn't know the first thing about Africa. If there really were such a thing as magic, she'd zap Melanie into an Egypt winter or a Maji fog—like walking through cold, wet satin—or, better yet, plop her down shivering in a Nairobi rainstorm with frogs squeezing under the door.

"Some summers are hotter than this one was, too," Melanie blabbed on. "Sometimes it's so muggy and hot that you think slugs could swim in your neck sweat. But you and Jakarta will think nothing of that."

"Don't be an ignoramus," Dakar said. Why didn't anybody *understand*?

Melanie flushed. "Pardoney moi for existing."

"Want to learn an African phrase I learned in boarding school?" Dakar asked glumly.

Of course Melanie did. "Repeat after me," Dakar said. "O-wa."

"O-wa."

"Ta-gu."

"Ta-gu." Melanie's voice was full of just the right amount of awe.

"Siam."

"Siam."

"Now say it fast," Dakar said.

Melanie rattled the words off proudly. For a moment there was a bleak silence. Then she said, "You're mean now that Jakarta came."

"At least I don't have purple hair."

"I can't believe you said that." Melanie glared at her. "That's it. No more chances. You stay away from me, and you stay away from my magic place."

As soon as Melanie ran off, Dakar felt ashamed. After all, she had to admit she was ignorant, too. She'd had no idea what Russells were.

In school she tried not to notice when she walked by Melanie and the girl with the purple hair. She was invisible. Or they were invisible. "Anyway, big, hairy deal," she told herself. She had Jakarta now, and she didn't mind slipping ghost-like through school. *That* she was used to. "Where were you?" she asked Jakarta at dinner.

"Researching the basketball team," Jakarta said. "They've already started the season. But I might still be able to get in." She grinned broadly. "The coach told me to come to practice this afternoon so he could take a look. I made about eleven shots in a row. Nobody passed to me—that's for sure. All of my shots were off rebounds that I had to risk my skin for."

"Think carefully before you fritter all your time away," Dad said. His voice sounded preoccupied. "I think you'll find sports in a North Dakota high school a lot different from in a small international school."

"When in Rome," Jakarta said. "Please pass the mushrooms and peas. What do you think, Dakar? Would I make an excellent Lady Wildcat?"

"You know," Dad said, "I got a call today from one of my friends at the MSF."

Dakar sat motionless with the dish of mushrooms and peas in midair. Médecins sans Frontières. Doctors Without Borders. Dad had worked on MSF teams lots of times before, including in Somalia and in the Sudan.

"He was talking about a terrible earthquake in Guatemala." Dad's voice was sorrowful. "The emergency rescue teams have done all they can. Now it's time to help the survivors." He shook his head. "What's taking your mom so long to get back here?"

"I know you want to leave," Jakarta said bitterly. "Just leave."

Dad looked at her in surprise. "I do want to leave, of course. The situation's desperate, and they need every pair of hands. But I won't leave the two of you alone."

"Oh, come on," Jakarta said. "Lots of people my age in East Africa are married at sixteen. It's not like I haven't taken care of Dakar before."

"Maybe I should then," Dad said.

Dakar couldn't read his tone. Was he serious?

"Good," Jakarta said. She pushed her chair back. "I think you should. I'm sure they need you."

"Don't worry about it. I'm sure your mom will be back soon."

Jakarta got to her feet. "Did it ever occur to you that maybe she doesn't want to come back?"

"No, it never did." His voice was firm and impatient. "And it doesn't now."

Dakar sat looking at the mushrooms and peas in her hand as once again Jakarta headed for the door. She finished her meal in silence and then wandered outside. She thought she knew where Jakarta had probably gone. As she got close to the park, she could see Jakarta on one of the basketball courts, practicing her moves on Pharo. Most of the time Jakarta didn't get past him, but every once in a while she could. Then she would crow and flap her arms. Dakar leaned into the fence and watched them facing each other, panting and glinty-eyed.

"Stay friendly, baby," Pharo said. "Come on."

Jakarta looked anything but friendly.

"Come on." Pharo wiggled his fingers at her. "Think you can get past me?"

Jakarta swayed lightly. A little right. A little left. Suddenly she moved, and he was right with her like a mirror, except that she wasn't going that direction after all, now that he was committed, and before Dakar could even figure out exactly what had happened, Jakarta was free and driving toward the basket, and the few spectators, standing around and half watching, were hooting joyously—"slippery as a soapy baby!" yelled one—and Dakar was laughing, without even meaning to, and imagining that it was she who was feeling that fine, shimmering tightness when every muscle is singing. She hadn't even known Jakarta could play basketball like this.

"Sloppy," Pharo said. But he was grinning. "You better take a break and work on dribbling with that left hand, hey? A three-year-old could take it away from you on the left side." As they walked by Dakar, he said, "My mom says, where have you been?"

Dakar walked home hearing the bounce of the basketball behind her.

Late that evening, after she finished her homework, she stuck her head into Jakarta's room and said, "Actually Coach Svedborg is going to kiss your feet."

"Think so?" Jakarta looked up eagerly. She patted her bed. "Come tell me all about him."

Dakar caught her breath. Mom and Jakarta

could be so much alike sometimes. "I don't know that much. Melanie said a few girls complain because he yells. But most of them worship him. They know he's yelling because he wants a winning basketball team for once." She felt sad remembering Melanie that day. Melanie saying, "You know what my cousin said? He said, 'What do those players expect? They're supposed to be *wildcats*, not tabby cats.'"

"So Coach Svedborg is a tough cookie?"

"I guess so." Dakar suddenly felt *elated*. If Jakarta got involved in basketball, she would surely stay. And what would Melanie think if Dakar were the sister of a Lady Wildcat?

Later she was almost asleep when Jakarta poked her head into her room. "Wish me luck," Jakarta said. "I've decided that tomorrow I'll go meet my nemesis." Jakarta grinned recklessly. "Think my nemesis will be prepared for the ordeal of meeting me?"

That night Dakar fell asleep to the lullaby of the thump, thump sound of Jakarta jumping rope. It wasn't "Barbry Allen." But it was still comforting.

In her dreams that night, False Dimitri was running after Catherine the Great, swinging a sword and screaming. Catherine hollered, "Stay friendly, baby."

In the morning Dakar woke up sweating and coughing. The first thing she did was make sure Dad was still there. "Going to the library again?" she asked him.

"Not today." He sounded distracted, but he smiled at her. "I'm driving into Minnesota to talk to some people about relief supplies for Guatemala."

"Oh." She was trying to think of something else to say, something useful and maybe even grand, when Jakarta clattered down the stairs.

"Come on," Jakarta said. "Hustle up, sweet one." So Dakar did.

With so little sleep, she was dragging herself through P.E. class when the school secretary called her out to tell her that she had a phone call. "Family emergency," the secretary said.

Dakar felt as though her feet had been swept out from under her and she'd landed flat on the mat. Mom? Or maybe Dad had gone into a hospital to consult about someone who was sick. Maybe he caught a virus that swept through the hospital so fast no one could stop it before everyone had collapsed in twitching heaps on the floor. She shuffle-ran most of the way to the office, glancing down all the halls to see if anyone mouthy was around to see her in her gym shorts.

"Dakar?" It was Jakarta.

"What's wrong?" It had to be something awful if Mom or Dad couldn't even talk to her themselves.

"I made it!" Jakarta said. "Coach just told me he's letting me on the basketball team."

"Jakarta!" Dakar put both hands on the phone and shook it hard. "Did you hear that? I just shook the phone. I wish it was your neck."

Jakarta laughed. "Sorry. Did I scare you? I had to tell them it was an emergency because otherwise they wouldn't get you out of class. And it *is* an emergency, don't you think? I not only made the team—I'm a starter."

Dakar glanced around. The secretary was talking to someone, but you never knew what secretaries could hear. "Hey, I've gotta go," she whispered. "I'm in the middle of P.E."

"One more thing," Jakarta said.

"All right, but hurry—because I have to get out of these stupid gym shorts before someone sees me."

"The rest of the team was all standing in the

gym when I walked in," Jakarta said. "And . . . they clapped. They clapped for me." Her voice was suddenly soaked with emotion. "They could have hated me for pushing my way in, but they didn't. It's so supaloaf to be part of a team again."

After school Dakar raced all the way home. She was checking Dad's closets, burrowing her nose into the incense smell, when she heard him drive up. She ran downstairs to hug him, squeezing his chest and strong arms as if she could hold him there.

The next few weeks blurred by. Every morning Dakar checked first for Dad. Every evening she hugged him. He hugged her back, but he looked sad and faraway. Most mornings, he got up early and drove to one or the other of the university libraries. He didn't sing anymore. His restlessness seemed to fill the house and spill out the edges.

"Shouldn't we start raking the leaves?" Dakar asked him. "They're almost covering the lawn."

He shook his head. "Let them rot and go into the soil and provide humus."

Dakar blinked, remembering the glossy grass under her fingers. Remembering Mom. "So leaves on the lawn are like wild hedges?"

At least that made him laugh. Then he tapped his fingers on the table for a few minutes and stared out the window. Finally he said, "When I was in college, I stayed with a family in Guatemala for a few weeks, and the father loved to sweep the yard. By the time he was done, there wasn't even one leaf. He would talk to me as he worked, while his small son dodged around our legs, giggling and pretending to play soccer. He said his people have been suffering since the conquistadores rode up three hundred years ago."

Dakar tried to think of something to say, but her mind felt as smooth and blank as the window glass.

Every time Mom called, she said Aunt Lily was doing a little bit better. Then she always went on to talk about harvest or something. One time she said, "Aunt Lily has been telling me stories about when she and Mother were little girls and would run two miles to confirmation class, where they loved to eat the peanut butter and syrup sandwiches for supper." Another time she said, "Aunt Lily and I have been looking through all of Mother's things." She never said anything about coming home.

Jakarta was no help. All she could think about

was basketball—how to improve her game and whether she had her footwork right. Maybe, Dakar finally decided, the cook would know what to tell her about the feeling that something big was crouched just inside the front door, waiting to gulp her down the minute she forgot to be scared.

The next morning she and Jakarta had gotten almost all the way to school when she realized that for the first time she hadn't even looked at Melanie's house. That was good. "I'm over her," Dakar said out loud as she trotted down the stairs and toward the kitchen.

Schiiick. Schiick.

She stopped. A strange woman was standing at the counter chopping tomatoes. "Where's the cook?"

"I'm the cook."

Dakar looked around anxiously. Nobody moved a knife the way *her* cook could. "But where's the real cook?"

She hated the way the woman chuckled. "You mean Ms. Plummer? Gone home. First time off she ever took since she started working for the district, she told me."

"Did she leave a message for anyone she called Africa child?"

"No," the woman said. "No message."

In English class Dakar rippled the pages of her book helplessly, staring at her desk while Ms. Olson explained, for the zillionth time, what a preposition was. Even when the whole class started complaining that it was too hard and stupid to tell when "to" was a preposition and when it wasn't, Dakar didn't look up. No one looked at Dakar, either. Wildebeests. Good thing she had an invisibility cloak.

After school she went for a walk. Everywhere she looked, leaves were chittering along the sidewalk, brushing against one another and piling in little heaps. Darkness came so early these days that Dakar was shivering in her sweater by the time she got home. Jakarta was lying on the couch tossing the basketball straight up in the air and catching it. "Pharo's coming for supper," she said. "I told him . . ." Her voice stumbled a second and then caught itself. "I told him to eat with us while his mom is gone because our mom and dad are gone, too."

Dakar stiffened. "Dad did it? He really went?" She wanted to howl. "When will he be back?"

Jakarta caught the basketball and held it still. "I'm sorry, Dakar. He and I got in another big argument, and he said he'd been thinking about things and realized . . . realized I was right. He said you and I were very resourceful, more resourceful than spoiled kids in the United States."

Dakar coughed. Her throat was filling up with sadness, but she refused to cry. "When is he going to come *back*?"

Jakarta pulled her down on the couch and gave her a hug. "Probably pretty soon. But you know how Dad is when he's helping with a humanitarian crisis. He gets completely involved, right? He loses track of everything, including—may I point out—time and his family." She frowned. "At least he had the decency not to write to Mom, because of course, she'd feel like she should sacrifice her time with Great-Aunt Lily."

Dakar tried to think exactly where Guatemala was. It couldn't be *that* far from North Dakota, could it?

"He gave me a credit card to use so we can buy things." Jakarta pulled it out of her pocket and waved it like a fan in front of her face. "Anyway, as I said, Pharo is going to eat with us tonight. Then he and I can practice basketball after supper."

"Where is Pharo's mom, anyhow?"

"Visiting her family. See, people do that. Don't be such a worrymeister."

Dakar sighed. She wanted to ask what Dad had said exactly and whether he'd given Jakarta any messages specifically for her. In fact, she wanted to wail like a little kid and kick the stupid universe in the knee for making the cook and Dad disappear on the same day. How unfair was that? "*Ayezosh*," she told herself. Maybe this was her chance to show Jakarta how brave she could be. Dad and Mom would both come back soon, wouldn't they? "How did basketball go?" she asked. If Jakarta saw that Dakar wasn't such a wart anymore, she would probably want to stay, too, and they'd all be together at last.

Jakarta grinned. "We lost today but we are on the edge of being so good. Coach moved me to point guard. It's going to make a world o' difference."

Dakar smiled back, caught in the glow. What a buff Jakarta was. She and Jakarta *were* resourceful, and, anyway, they'd been almost on their own in boarding school, hadn't they? "What do you think of him?"

"Coach? He kinda reminds me of Dad, which is ironic. Pretty intense around the eyes. Here." She jumped up and tossed the basketball to Dakar. "Now throw it back. You be the guard."

It felt good to have something to do. Dakar waved her arms and bounced wildly on the balls of her feet, determined to stop Jakarta. Up on her toes. Watch . . . watch . . . but Jakarta faked and was around her in an instant. Dakar slammed her fist against her thigh in frustration.

"Watch my stomach, not my eyes," Jakarta said, grinning at her. "Stomachs don't lie."

"Maybe I could help you like I did with soccer," Dakar said. It would make time go by, anyway.

"Sure." Jakarta hesitated. "I'm sorry I've been such a barracuda and maybe drove Dad off or something."

Dakar wanted to say something mean, something angry. But how would that help anything? "It's okay," she said sadly. "He probably would have gone, anyway."

"No, it isn't okay." Jakarta sat down, dribbling with her left hand. "We're supposed to take turns making supper. I'll just do it for a while, though, if you want."

Dakar nodded. Jakarta kept dribbling. She was getting pretty good with her left hand. It was going to be some kind of miracle in reverse if Jakarta didn't get that team on a roll.

"By the way," Jakarta said, "I don't think you

should tell anyone that Mom and Dad are gone. Not *anyone*, okay? I have no idea what the laws are like here, but I'd hate to wake up one morning and have us in a foster home or something."

Dakar imagined she could hear moth wings brushing against the kitchen window. She wished she could ask Jakarta what exactly was going to happen to them. She wished she could ask about that day when she'd been so sure she heard Jakarta's voice. But how would she even start?

FROM DAKAR'S BOOK
OF LISTS AND THOUGHTS

Some things we need to learn how to do that
we've never (or hardly ever) done

1. Cook suppers.
2. Wash clothes.
3. Buy groceries.
4. Vacuum.
5. Clean windows and stuff.

I wonder what I'm forgetting. How ironic that Jakarta's here now and they're gone. Here's a horrible thought. What if my quest brought Jakarta back but somehow, without knowing it, I made some terrible bargain with the universe? I think the saddest story in the whole Bible is the one about Jephthah. He told God that if he won a great battle, whatever he first saw when he came to his house would be a sacrifice. And behold, his only daughter came out to meet him with timbrels and with dance. He tore his clothes and said to his daughter, Alas. You have brought me very low. As much as I love you, I cannot take back my vow. Every year after that the daughters of Israel went out for four days to lament the daughter of Jephthah.

Did I do something that brought Jakarta back but sent Mom and Dad away?

THIRTEEN

Nighttimes were going to be the worst. "Be sensible," Dakar wrote in her lists and thoughts book, gripping the pen tightly to keep her fingers from shaking. "What's going to *get* you here? A lion? A deadly mamba snake? If a person was going to break into the house, what good would Mom and Dad have been, anyway?" She promised herself she wouldn't tell Jakarta what a worrywart she was being.

The next afternoon she had to walk home by herself because Jakarta had practice. When she stepped into the house, a swoosh of silence met her. "Dad?" she said out loud. But of course, he didn't answer. She always worried so much about Dad when he was gone.

"Foo on you," she told his face in the picture that hung by the table. "We'll have fun without you." She rooted around in the cupboard until she found a cupcake mix.

Okay. Just follow the directions. How hard could it be? Later, when they were eating supper, she told herself it had been fun, even if she had only made macaroni and cheese from a box with the cupcakes for celebration. It was fun doing homework in the living room while Jakarta typed e-mail messages to her Nairobi friends.

"E-mail message from Dad," Jakarta said.

"Where?" Dakar jumped up. "Let me see."

"It just says he's there and fine," Jakarta said. "Exhausted. Kinda sad. There's an e-mail address where someone can get him if we have an emergency. He loves us."

Looking over Jakarta's shoulder, Dakar read it for herself. Jakarta was right. That was exactly what it said. Even though Dad said he'd be out in the camps and not near a computer, Dakar made Jakarta type an e-mail message right away saying that they loved him, too. She felt guilty for saying foo to him. For being mad.

The closer it got to bedtime, the more Dakar found herself stalling. "Did you like the family you were staying with in Kenya?" she asked when she'd finished the rewrite of her paper on Roman battle strategies and there was absolutely no reason not to go upstairs.

Jakarta was stretched out on the floor, rolling the basketball with one hand and balancing her history book on her chest with the other. "Sure," she said. "Malika was my best friend at school, anyway."

Dakar forced a smile. A pure-hearted person wouldn't feel jealous when Jakarta said things like that.

Jakarta sat up and tossed her history book into the wastebasket. "Two points!" She laughed. "A couple of days after school started, Malika came running downstairs to say there was a snake in her computer." Jakarta started to laugh harder, so that for a minute she had trouble telling the story. She and Malika had gotten a bag and stick and chased the snake around the room until they got it into the bag. Then they managed to pour the snake into a jar. "It didn't really want to go," Jakarta explained, "but we shook the bag, trying to make sure the unzipped part stayed over the opening of the jar, and finally the snake dropped in. We thought it was the little black house snake her brother had brought home over vacation that had managed to escape, but Mr. Jenotte pounded it into us last year that you should always assume a snake is poisonous until you know for sure, so we were careful with it. Guess what?"

Dakar shook her head. "Don't tell me. Shut up, Jakarta. It's almost bedtime. Don't say it, okay?"

"It's all right," Jakarta said, giving her a big grin. "It wasn't a puff adder or something. It was a white-lipped snake, not one of the kind that can kill you. It would have made us sick but not dead."

"Just shut up about the snake," Dakar said sulkily. "I'm going to bed." She was halfway up the stairs when she hesitated and turned around. "Changed my mind," she said. "I'll just lie here on the couch. You can read your history."

For a few minutes she lay still, listening to Jakarta turning pages. Just as she started trying to think of something else to ask Jakarta, the phone rang. Dakar dashed to the kitchen phone, calling, "Get the extension in the living room."

Mom sounded breathless and faint. "It was a long walk over here," she said. "But the stars were astonishing, and the stubble crackled under my feet. I felt as if I were walking across an island in the middle of nowhere, with the sea hissing all around me and curling up the beaches."

Dakar started to say "Mom," but Jakarta cut her off. "I'm point guard for the basketball team now, Mom," she said.

Mom's voice got stronger then. She said all the right, excited things, and started telling Jakarta stories about her own basketball-playing grandmother. Dakar put her hand over the receiver and waved to get Jakarta's attention. "We should tell her about Dad," she mouthed.

Jakarta shook her head firmly. "What was their court like?" she asked Mom.

"Well, according to Aunt Lily, they played on a dirt court that was smooth and hard from all the pounding feet. They would ride to the other schools in a wagon pulled by horses with a canvas cover over the top. It took all afternoon to go and come home." Mom stopped. "Can you imagine? And isn't this a coincidence? Aunt Lily and I were just talking about it this afternoon."

"Why not?" Dakar said out loud to Jakarta.

"Tell you later," Jakarta mouthed back. To Mom, she said, "Do you know what Great-Grandma's practices were like?"

"I'll ask Aunt Lily," Mom said. "Can I talk to your dad?"

"He's not here," Jakarta said.

"Oh." Mom suddenly sounded sad and faraway. "Well, tell him I called."

As soon as Dakar hung up the phone, she started to pout. "Why *not*?" she wailed.

"Come on, Dakar," Jakarta said. "Don't you think

Mom deserves some happiness, too? You and I will be fine, won't we?"

Dakar didn't answer. She went over to the window and breathed hot air against the glass, making a steamy O. She drew a sad face on the glass with her finger. "And I don't care if it's hard to clean," she whispered resentfully.

"Come on," Jakarta said. "I'll make you hot cocoa. Remember how I would melt chocolate bars on my hot plate at boarding school and sneak milk from the dining room so I could make you hot cocoa when you were sad and couldn't sleep?"

They sat at the table, and Dakar slurped her cocoa on purpose. She had to think. The family was more apart than ever, and now she didn't even have the cook to give her advice. Somehow she'd have to come up with a new plan completely by herself.

"I remember when I was in sixth grade in boarding school," Jakarta said gently. "I thought if I could only get back to Mom, she could make everything right again. But when you're as old as I am, you'll realize moms need things, too. Maybe she needs her mother."

"Her mother is dead," Dakar said sullenly.

Jakarta didn't say anything.

"Oh." Dakar was mad at herself for being such a baby. "You mean, Aunt Lily?"

"Yeah. Aunt Lily."

Dakar looked up at the family picture on the wall, and Dad's eyes bore into her. "You are the hero of your own life," he was saying.

"Don't give up," she told herself. "Don't give up, O ye of little faith." Okay, but what next? She'd been making herself be brave because she thought Jakarta might want to stay around her if she were brave, the type of person who would handle a white-lipped snake and laugh about it. But what would Mom want? What might be the key to bringing Mom home? What would Odysseus do? He thought up all kinds of ideas when he was trapped by the Cyclops or had to go between Scylla and Charybdis. Or what did Cleopatra do when she was only fourteen and her beloved father was banished and her older sister was about to have her killed any day?

"Do you think Mom is ever coming back?" she said. "Maybe the Allalonestone got her again."

Jakarta shook her head, then reached over and gave a piece of Dakar's hair a little tug. "I hope not. I think she's sailing right along the top of the water on one of those boats we used to make for the water babies. The hoodies can't get her and pull her under as long as she stays on the boat. Pretty soon the river will swirl her right back to our door."

"How did you first make up the water babies, anyway?" Dakar asked.

Jakarta looked surprised. "Don't you remember? It's a book. Mom read it to us, but you were probably too little to understand it then. There were lots of words and things I didn't understand myself. But later I read it out loud to you. And we made up a game about it. We cleared a path down in that place where the vines were. I used to make you swing on the vines to be sure they would hold us. Remember?"

Dakar remembered the vines and how honored she used to feel when Jakarta would tell her that it was an important job to be the Vine Tester. After Jakarta left, Dakar taught Wondemu to be a Vine Tester, too. They took turns being Vine Testers. She'd always felt sorry for Jakarta that Jakarta was too big to be one. Now she realized that she'd been naive and that Jakarta had been saving her own tail by making Dakar test all the vines first.

"We named places along the path to go with the book," Jakarta said. "The Other End of Nowhere and the Shiny Wall and the White Gate that was never opened and finally Mother Carey's Haven, where the good whales go when they die. Don't you remember that?"

Mother Carey's Haven. Something was really important about that. What was it? Dakar shook her head, frustrated that she couldn't catch the slippery memory.

"Do you remember that Mom would read books to us when we were in the bathtub? We had to save water in Maji because it always had to be heated up on the woodstove."

"Yes," Dakar said. "I remember that." She remembered Jakarta or Dad soaping her hair, the sting of the soap in her eyes, the soft light of the kerosene lamp. She remembered running down the hall in her nightgown afterward, her feet cold on the concrete, leaping so that the lion that hid under her bed wouldn't grab her.

"After a while we didn't play on that path anymore," Jakarta said. "I don't really remember when we quit playing the game about getting to Mother Carey's Haven. But the first time we went with Dad down to the waterfall and saw those fern tips, I knew instantly that they were water babies."

Dakar rubbed her arms. It was chilly in the

house. Did she and Jakarta know anything about how to turn on the heat when it got really cold? What if they had to wrap up in blankets with their arms around each other to try to keep warm? What if Mom and Dad came home and found them huddled together in bed, frozen solid? "Did you ever know where the water babies went after we couldn't see them anymore?" she asked.

"Not really. On down the river."

Dakar got up and dumped the rest of her cocoa in the sink. Her stomach was jumping, and she felt slightly sick.

She couldn't even remember now why she'd gotten so determined that day to follow the water babies to the very end of their journey. That afternoon, just like every other time, the boats had gone into a deep pool where they turned slow, loopy circles. Then the current began to slowly pull them out the far side of the pool. "Come on," she'd shouted to Wondemu over the roar of the water. "We have to follow them."

They'd had to push and fight through the thick bushes. If Wondemu weren't there to help her, she would never have gotten through. When they couldn't make the bushes budge anymore, they got down on their hands and knees and crawled, heads down, pushing through with their arms. Suddenly the bushes gave way. Dakar could still feel the lurch, the way her breath fluttered in her throat as she stumbled out and saw that they were right at the edge of a cliff.

With a huge roaring that made talking impossible, the water babies' river spun away from the rocks and flung itself hundreds and hundreds of feet down. When Dakar and Wondemu inched forward on their stomachs and stared into dizzying space, she could see it shattering into droplets on the rocks far, far below.

FOURTEEN

That night Dakar dreamed she was trapped in the Allalonestone. She couldn't move her arms and legs. Grayish black flat stone was all around her, and she was utterly and forever alone. She woke up panting and rummaged in her drawer for the candle and matches. "Come back," she whispered as she stared into the flame. "Come back. Come back. Come back."

When school was over that afternoon, she didn't even go into the silent house. Instead, she hunted around in the garage until she found a rake. Mom wanted picket-fence neat? Fine. It was time for one of those quests like the ones where the princess has to pick up a thousand pieces of corn before nightfall. Dakar carried the rake outside, studied the yard, and then picked a spot and began to coax the leaves into a pile.

She raked for what she was pretty sure was hours and hours. Leaves were still dancing down, and they got caught in her hair and sweater, but she didn't care. She got a blister on her hand, and she didn't care about that, either. From time to time she stopped and counted how many piles she had made. She loved raking. Today was just exactly the way autumn was in the books. She stared up at the two-story house, and for a change it was looking back at her, smiling and nodding.

Sooner or later she'd given each of their houses a name because they came to remind her of certain people. The apartment in Egypt had made her think of a picture of teenage Elvis Presley, surly and full of itself. So she named it Elvis. Some days the house in Nairobi was Cleopatra, and some days it was Donbirra. Finally she called it Donbirra Cleopatra. Elegant, with unknowable eyes. The house in Maji was best, of course, because they stayed there the longest and it felt most like home. She named it Gabriel, after the angel. The Bible didn't say that Gabriel was the angel who said, "Behold, I bring you good tidings of great joy, which shall be to all people," but Dakar was sure he was. Angels had to be team players because they hardly ever got their individual names mentioned.

She was the only one who got that attached to most of the houses. Dad didn't like cities, and once they left Maji, he seemed to hover uneasily, like some exotic moth, over Elvis and Donbirra Cleopatra, mostly escaping to places where his favorite people—peasants, farmers, nomads—lived. Mom didn't like cities, either, and chose to live in them only so Jakarta and Dakar wouldn't have to go to boarding school.

What was this house's name? She squinted up at it, moved to the other side of the yard, and looked at it again. It didn't seem able to communicate, maybe because it was only a shell without Dad's energy and Mom's warmth. No matter how many different angles she studied, the name didn't come. A shout startled her, and she looked up. It was Jakarta and Pharo, jogging home.

"You're making more work for yourself than you need to," Jakarta called. "Dad said just ignore them."

"I like to rake," Dakar called back. "I never had a chance to do it before."

At the supper table Jakarta said, "You should at least wait until all the leaves are down. You're just going to have to do it all over again."

"You're crazy, man," Pharo told her. "My mom always tells me I have to rake. The day she left she said, 'You be sure to rake for those people you stay with.' Your sister says you don't have to rake, and you still rake."

But she did have to. They just didn't understand. That was okay, though. People hardly ever did understand heroes like Gilgamesh and their quests. "Where *are* you staying?" she asked Pharo.

"With Aaron Johnson. From the team. I'd already been overnight there lots of times. Every day I go to the apartment and water my mama's plants."

Dakar sneaked a quick frown at Jakarta. "Does your mama call you all the time?"

"Nah, man." Pharo chuckled. "She's not in a place of any telephones. Besides, the Johnsons are lawyers. Nothing scares them. And my mama has had no life to herself for years. Why should she spend this trip worrying about me?"

Jakarta lifted her eyebrows at Dakar with a look that said, "See?" To Pharo, she said, "Lawyers, huh? Well, don't tell the Johnsons anything about us." Her voice got even more stern. "Or if your mom comes back. Don't tell."

He laughed. "Hey, keep it friendly, baby. Long as things are okay here, I got no need to be blabbing. But if you need anything, you find me right away."

Jakarta pulled the baked chicken out of the oven and put it on the table with a flourish. "We're doing pretty well, aren't we?" she said. "For a bunch of motherless chicks."

"We haven't bought groceries yet," Dakar pointed out. "Or done your smelly, sweaty laundry. Or figured out how to turn on the heat."

"Pharo can show us about the heat, can't you?" Jakarta said.

"I'll look at your furnace," Pharo said. "Hope it's like ours. Anyone else want a glass of H-two-O?"

"Oops. Guess we need something to drink." Jakarta reached behind her for the mug tree. "Did you know that elements like hydrogen and oxygen were forged in the hearts of stars? Hey, tomorrow's going to be a great game. You guys are coming, aren't you?"

The Lady Wildcats, Dakar saw when she picked up the program on her way into the gym the next afternoon, were more than halfway through their season, and they had won a few more games than they had lost. She found Jakarta's name and height and then looked around. About thirty people were scattered in the gym.

"Let's go!" someone shouted. A cheerleader did backflips across the gym floor. Everyone stood for the school song and the national anthem. Then the starters were introduced. Each player ran to the middle of the court as her name was called, and there was great slapping of hands and hips.

"Go, Jakarta," Dakar said softly as the two centers squared off for the jump.

"How are they doing?" Dakar asked Pharo halfway through the game, when the gym was juicy with sweat and panting.

He shook his head. "Little wobbly," he said. "Just a little bit wobbly." The Wildcats weren't used to having someone like Jakarta at point guard, he explained. "She's more aggressive than they're used to, and she passes harder. Hey!" He jumped to his feet. "Wake up out there." He sat back down. "See that? It was a great pass, but Emily wasn't expecting it. She'll get it, though. If she doesn't, Jakarta will start putting it in herself." He pulled a candy bar from his pocket and offered Dakar the first bite. "Take it yourself, Jakarta," he hollered as he chewed. "Put that biscuit in the basket."

The Wildcats lost, 54–50. After the game, though, the team huddled together, and Dakar heard someone say, "We'll get the next one."

"Jakarta, you were high scorer again," the coach barked. "Let's see if we can set some picks and get you open for more shots next time."

"Your sister is some player," Pharo said to Dakar. "Did you see the way she inhales rebounds?"

That night Mom called again. "Aunt Lily says her mom told her that they learned basketball by watching the boys practice." Mom's voice sounded faraway and fragile, and Dakar pressed her ear to the phone. "Grandma could make layups and also long shots. And they wore blue bloomers and blue middy tops with white sailor collars and tennis shoes." Mom laughed softly, and her voice was suddenly sad. "It was all such a long time ago, though. That's really all Aunt Lily can remember."

"Come home," Dakar longed to say. "I'm trying to make the lawn and everything just the way you'll like it." But she didn't.

"Are you all right?" she asked.

"Some days I walk for hours through the fields," Mom said. "I almost imagine I'm a little girl and my parents will be there when I get home. Well, I love you guys. Could I talk to your dad?"

"He's out saving the world," Jakarta said.

Dakar squeezed her lips into a thin, disappointed line, and she shook her head.

"What?" Jakarta mouthed. "It's the truth." Into the phone, she said, "We're fine."

Dakar shook her head again. Did Jakarta really

want to be kind to Mom, or was she just being stubborn to prove something to Dad?

She hung up and started slowly up the stairs, sliding her hand along the banister. Why didn't Mom ask where Dad was? Then they would have to tell her, right? They couldn't just be False Dimitris to Mom, and if they told her, she'd have to come home. For a moment Dakar felt a stubbornness to match Jakarta's. Maybe she should say something no matter what Jakarta thought.

Nah. Jakarta and Pharo would think she was such a tree fungus for not caring about Mom. She had to be *stalwart*. She had to ignore all these feelings thumping on her, making her feel like a drum. She had to be brave for Jakarta *and* Mom— and hope the leaf quest somehow worked.

"You will not fear the terror of the night," she told herself as she climbed. "Nor the arrow that flies by day. Nor the pestilence . . . the pestilence . . ." She turned around and went back down. "Can I sleep in your room?"

Jakarta looked up. "Okay. But you have to take the little bed by the door."

"Fine," Dakar said, her voice shaky with relief. "That just means anything that comes in the window will get you first."

The Lady Wildcats won their next three games. Dakar loved to watch. The gym was always nearly empty except for the cheerleaders and a few parents, but she didn't care about that. She just liked to watch Jakarta running up and down the floor, her long hair caught in a ponytail or braids that bounced every time her feet hit the floor. Sometimes Jakarta yelled out numbers as she ran. Sometimes she just waved her teammates into place or gave them hand signals, and they obediently fanned out this way and that, doing a delicate dance. "Go, Jakarta!" Dakar learned to scream. She hadn't felt this good since they left Africa.

She got to know each player's name. Emily, Shannon, Andrea, Kinsey, and Jakarta were the usual starters. Laura came off the bench, sometimes midway through the first quarter, but immediately if Emily started making wild passes. Jen and Beth came in if the Wildcats were either way ahead or hopelessly behind. A few other players mostly warmed the bench.

"Take that shot," Coach Svedborg sometimes yelled at Jakarta. Once in a time-out he hollered,

"You need to be more selfish. If the shot's there, take it."

Dakar didn't like to hear him yelling at Jakarta. But in the second half Jakarta made twenty points. Dakar waited for her to change and walked her home. "You were supaloaf today," she said.

"I felt supaloaf." Jakarta gave her a look of fierce joy. "It feels like every nerve and muscle is tingling when I'm out there." She paused. "All those memories that stick to me like red Kenya dust . . . well . . . when I'm playing, I don't think of Africa or my friends or *anything* else except me and the ball and my teammates."

The next morning Jakarta's face stared up from the front of the sports page. "She could be an effective post player, she's our best perimeter player, she can break a press, she's a fabulous passer," the coach was quoted as saying. "She just does so many things. And she makes her teammates better because she likes to pass. I actually have to get on her about shooting more."

Two days later the university television station sent out a crew. That night the team and Dakar all went to Emily's house to have pizza and watch.

"Near the end of the season the Lady Wildcats

are playing with ice in their veins and fire in their bellies," the reporter began.

"With Jakarta, we have a whole new look," Emily said into the mike. "She refuses to lose. She doesn't like to lose at anything. From the first day she practiced with us, she was kicking everybody when we were running sprints." On the screen Jakarta let loose a long three and it swished in.

Dakar ate her pizza, shyly watching the girls laughing and giving each other high-fives. "Look, Mom," she wanted to holler. "Look, Dad. Jakarta's on television."

The next evening Dakar was surprised to look around and realize that the bleachers were more than half full. The gym quivered with noise every time the girls were bringing the ball down the court. It dropped into silence when a Wildcat was making a free throw. The funniest thing was what happened after Jakarta made her fourth three-point shot. Someone started it up and others took up the chant: "Tarzan. Tarzan. Tarzan."

Dakar's invisibility cloak had holes in it now. "Is that Tarzan girl your sister?" kids asked her. Kids she didn't even know. She tried to give them Donbirra eyes of eggshell calm, even though she often felt just like what the reporter had said about the Lady Wildcat team—either ice or fire or both.

By this time the leaves were mostly off except for some pale lichen green leaves in a little tree in front. While Dakar waited for more leaves to come down, she carried armloads of wood into the house. When the fireplace box was full and she still didn't have any more leaves to rake, she figured out how to use the vacuum cleaner. At least it made some noise in the house. The next day, when Jakarta had an away game, she walked to the store to read labels and then buy dust spray and glass cleaner for her smudges. Then, rather than spend time in the empty house, she sat in the gym and watched Jakarta practice.

Sometimes Jakarta shot three-point shots, making one after the other, moving steadily around the key. "I want to be able to make it from anywhere," she told Dakar. Sometimes she practiced jump shots or left-handed layups. Saturday, when almost nobody was in the gym yet, Jakarta stood just inside the free throw line and threw the ball, over and over, to a blond girl standing near the basket. Over and over the girl shot. Neither one of them moved, and the girl never missed.

Dakar began to feel dizzy, as if she were caught in the loop of a movie. The blond girl wasn't one of the starters. Dakar had never even noticed her sitting on the bench. There was something weird about the way she was standing. But she sure could make baskets from that spot.

When the rest of the team started coming in, Dakar wandered back home to see if there was anything to rake. The leaves from the little tree in the middle were finally coming down, dusting one spot on the lawn with a light green cloak. It didn't take long to rake them up. Most of the leaves had been picked up by the town's trucks. Only two neat piles remained. "I've made your lawn look so nice," she told the house. "Won't you tell me your name?" The house smiled enigmatically.

Dakar walked back to the gym. Two practice teams were scrimmaging. Coach Svedborg ran up and down the court, red-faced, looking as if he thought he could see everything if he could always be right there, close enough. "Lollipop passes," he shouted. "You'll just be *handing* the ball to the other team with passes like that. Gift-wrapped. Here you go, ma'am."

Dakar wondered how he had enough breath to shout this much and run, too. Emily faked a move to the left, but her defender wasn't fooled. She flicked at the ball and stole it. Suddenly everyone was thundering down toward the other basket.

The B team point guard took the shot from about the free throw line. The ball wobbled around the rim. Even Dakar could see it was clearly coming off. Jakarta was in there, jostling, elbowing. She was leaping. Hands were everywhere, but somehow, even though she wasn't the tallest player, it was Jakarta's hands that were pulling the ball down, tucking it in as she swung her elbows. Then she was dribbling down the court, two steps ahead of everyone.

"Go in!" Coach Svedborg screamed. "Take it on in. Finish it off."

But Jakarta didn't. With her nearest defender still two steps away, Jakarta dished the basketball to Emily. *Swish*. Emily laid the ball in the basket.

"That was *sweet*," Jakarta said, grinning. Her hair was coming out of its braids, and sweat flew everywhere as she shook her head. "Really sweet."

"*Not* sweet," Coach bellowed. "We can't afford to lose another game. Take those shots, Jakarta. Don't take stupid chances."

"Right," Jakarta said. "Next time." But Dakar saw her grin at Emily as she turned away.

"Aren't you scared of Coach Svedborg?" Dakar asked when they were eating supper with Pharo.

"No. What's he going to do to me?"

"That's right," Pharo said. "Jakarta is his star girl. What's he going to do to his star girl, hey?"

"That's not it," Jakarta snapped. Pharo laughed. "I'm just trying to build a tight team," Jakarta said. "Everyone needs a team."

"He sure sounded mad today," Dakar said.

Pharo shrugged. "You can't be the hero if you can't be the goat."

"That's right," Jakarta said. "Coach Svedborg doesn't scare me. The only thing that scares me is not getting my English paper done. Not with an away game Friday."

"She'll let you turn it in late," Pharo said.

"I don't think so," Jakarta said. "She's already made one exception for my pathetic self."

"So. Skip our shoot-around tonight?" Pharo asked.

"Never." Jakarta whirled on him, and he laughed and held up his arms as if he needed to save himself from attack.

"Who was that girl I saw you practicing with today?" Dakar asked.

Jakarta hesitated. "Sharyn. I'm not even sure why she made the team."

"Yes, you know, hey?" Pharo said. "Someone felt sorry for her. That's why they let that girl on to the team. She's a hard worker, but she was born with something wrong with her foot. She's never going to play in a game. Never, never, never."

"She's got that one excellent shot, though," Jakarta said. "Too bad she can't just park under the basket and shoot it. Don't you ever feel bad about the girls Coach calls the blue-collar players, who show up with their lunch boxes even though they don't get any glory time? Why shouldn't I work with her?"

"Keep it friendly, baby," Pharo said. "I didn't say anything."

"I'm going out to see if there's anything more to rake," Dakar said, even though she knew there wasn't.

Pharo shook his head. "You're crazy, too," he said. "Snow is going to be here and cover those leaves up. Maybe even tonight. I feel it."

"Snow?" Dakar shook her head in disbelief.

"Right after we shoot around," Pharo said, "I'm looking at the furnace. Then I'm taking the two of you to a store. Gotta get scarves, gloves, Russell pants. Act like a babe in the woods when it comes to winter, and you could lose a finger." He waggled his fingers meaningfully at Jakarta.

"Okay, okay," Jakarta said. "Don't get in a twist. It's only October."

"Yeah," Dakar said. "Quit trying to scare us. It's nowhere near winter yet."

FIFTEEN

"Please. Not snow." Dakar peered out the window of her room later that evening with her new winter clothes all lying on the bed. Pharo had said the furnace was fine, but what did he actually know about furnaces? What if it coughed a bunch of carbon monoxide into the air and they went to sleep and never woke up? Or what if so much snow came down that they couldn't get out? What if the snow was up to their second-floor windows and they slowly starved to death? Before she went into Jakarta's room to sleep, she lit a candle and whispered into the flame, "Come home. Come home. Come home. Come home." Oops. Too close. That last *h* blew the candle out.

The next day felt like walking through glue. But every time Dakar glanced out the windows, she didn't see anything that looked like snow. Ha, she thought when they'd made it safely and snowlessly through the morning and most of the afternoon. She picked up a couple of the yellowish leaves and put them on top of the pile. Pharo wasn't right. She knew it. But the sky was a strange, soft gray, and the dark arms of the trees looked bleak and bare against it. Could winter possibly come this soon?

She tried to imagine what it would be like to see snowflakes floating down. What did snow actually and truly feel like when you touched it? Besides cold? She was pretty sure it was Egypt where Mom first read that snow poem out loud, because Dakar had a blurred memory of looking out the window at a yellow-and-beige world, imagining palm trees reaching up to catch handfuls of snow. She and Jakarta had pestered Mom with question after question. Did snow really clump on branches and pile so high that you had to dig a path to get through it? What was it like to float down a hill on a sled, your fingers tingling in your mittens?

In Maji they'd begged Mom to read the poem every night for a while. Finally, when the workers were cutting the grass on the hill behind the house, squatting to slide their hand scythes through handful after handful, leaving the grass lying in clumps to dry, she and Jakarta had come up with a snow poem plan. It wasn't easy finding the cardboard, but somehow Jakarta had managed.

For hours, they polished the pieces with handfuls of dried grass. Then they built grass paths down the hill. They spent one glorious day climbing the hill and sliding down on their cardboard sleds, over and over, until Jakarta decided to try a piece of tin, instead of the cardboard, and gashed her arm open. That put an end to the snow game, but for that one day, every time Dakar swooshed down the hill, she wondered if this was anything like snow. Now she was going to find out.

Could you run in snow? Toss it like confetti? Giddy with questions, Dakar leaped into the pile of leaves, laughing and throwing the leaves. Suddenly she stopped. No. Wait. If snow came down like confetti, it would cover up the lawn. Had she done all that work for nothing?

"Waaaaait," she hollered up at the sky, feeling foolish.

But the sky didn't wait. When Dakar woke up and looked out the window the next morning, she knew that Pharo had been right. Winter was dancing its way into town like a juggler pulling silk scarves from the sky, and the leaves would be covered with snow before Mom ever had a chance to see how tidy and safe she had made everything look.

She walked glumly downstairs and poured milk onto cereal, watching it splash over the cereal the way the snow would cover her leaves while she was in school. What was Mom doing right this minute? What about Dad? Was Dad missing them? Was he missing Mom? Probably he was working, too, and saving too many lives to think about missing anything at all. He was Donbirra's father in reverse. He loved his daughters, but he loved his work even more.

"Doesn't it bother you that Dad gets caught up in trying to save the world and forgets about us?" she asked Jakarta. Out the window she could see that the snow was now thick as a Maji fog. Good thing Pharo had made them get all that winter stuff.

"Not really. I think my real dad was the same way."

Dakar was shocked. Jakarta had never said those words before. Real. Dad. "Did Mom ever tell you more about *him*?" she asked cautiously. She wondered if Jakarta ever thought about the letter waiting for her when she turned eighteen.

"Not much. She said my real dad and Dad saw an accident when they were going out to look at some temple ruins. They turned around and were going back to help when another car hit them. My real dad was on the side of the car that got hit, and he died instantly."

Dakar stirred her cereal bleakly. Mushy. What if Dad had gotten killed, too? One thing she did *not* miss in Kenya was the driving: people slamming around, darting or blundering their way in and out, and saying *enshallah*, meaning that if God wanted them to die, they would die, and if God wanted them to live, they would live, so why bother to look before pulling out into a busy street? Addis Ababa was bad, too, but cars went faster in Nairobi, and there were more terrible accidents.

Probably Guatemala was another country of bad traffic, and maybe that was just the least of Dad's dangers. What if an unstable building toppled over and squashed him? What if deadly cholera started sweeping through the camps? Or some other loathsome disease from too many people and too little clean water and food?

She just *had* to think of something else to try. Jama was just a runt whose two older brothers called him things like son of a hyena, but he had saved Donbirra from the crocodile. She couldn't quit trying to get the family back together, no matter how many hoodies or how much snow tried to stop her.

All the way to school Dakar felt cold and wet. Snow kept creeping down the back of her neck, and she couldn't figure out how to use the scarf to keep it out. The wind had painted a skunk stripe of white on all the trees, and now it blew refrigerator air against her cheeks. When they got near Melanie's house, she stared at Melanie's windows. Three lights were on, and the house looked cozy and charmed. She looked closely for any movement, a shadow. Nothing.

With every step, her leg brushed against the cold denim of her jeans and made her shiver. Homesickness for East Africa trickled through her like a slow, sweet ache. "Don't forget the Nairobi eye fly," she told herself firmly. If you brushed at it and accidentally squashed it on your skin, it left ulcers. "Don't forget ugly Nairobi frogs." Last year, after the huge October rains, Yusef told them to be sure to block up the kitchen door against frogs. Sure enough, within a half hour, three big ones were squeezing their slimy swamp bodies under the door, and these weren't sweet Maji frogs, either, but sewer frogs. Mom got five out of the pantry. Jakarta counted fifty in the back entryway.

All fifty of those frogs would have been in the house if she and Jakarta and Mom hadn't been home to stuff plastic bags in the crack under the door. Yes, every place had its bad-weather agonies.

That morning one of the announcements over the intercom was about how the Lady Wildcats were about to qualify for regionals. Dakar pretended to hunt for something in her desk. "Look for the schedule on the board inside the high school door," the high school assistant principal said. "It's time to get out and support those roaring Lady Wildcats."

"Tell your sister good luck," Ms. Olson said.

Dakar blushed. Kids were looking. But for once their eyes didn't say *ferenji, mzungu, khawaaga*. She gave the class a shy smile back, holding the moment in her mind, sweet and bitter as pomegranate seeds.

When the end-of-class bell rang, she rushed out, still feeling flustered, and almost ran smack into Melanie, who wasn't looking where she was going because she was talking to two girls. One was Ms. Purple Hair. How long would it take for Melanie to have purple streaks in her own silvery white hair? Melaniethefollower. Off to follow someone else.

"Whoa—kid-hey," Purple Hair said. "You're Jakarta's sister, right?"

Dakar's eyes flickered to Melanie. But Melanie didn't say a word.

"Yeah," Dakar said. "That's right."

She felt ready to fight. Or ready to run. But all the girl said was, "We were just talking about how she's going to take the girls' basketball team to state. I don't think they'll win state, but wouldn't it be cool if they could? We've never had a girls' basketball team that even got to regionals."

"My cousin says they're definitely going to state," Melanie said.

Dakar looked at Melanie with a sudden longing. Maybe Melanie would say something about having gotten to meet Jakarta.

"*I* can't wait to see them play Bear Lake," the third girl said. "Bear Lake beats us in everything."

"Me, too," Melanie said. "But you know what? My cousin said the mongo important thing is that Jakarta is going to set the girls' school record for the most points in a regular season, and she didn't even play the whole season. She'll have her name on the wall with all the other Wildcat heroes, and the record will stay on the books for a long, long time. Maybe *forever*."

Dakar tried to squeeze something out of her mouth, but nothing came. "Come to my house this afternoon and tell me everything," she wanted to say to Melanie. Or, "Let's have another sleep-over at your house. I know a lot of other stories."

But she couldn't. How long would it be before Melanie found out that both Mom and Dad were gone? And Melanie's mom was just the type to think she and Jakarta needed foster care.

Okay, Dakar thought as she walked on. A mongo important thing, Melanie's cousin had said. What if Mom knew how well Jakarta was doing? Would she come home to help cheer Jakarta to victory? If Mom wouldn't come home for that, what was the chance she would ever come home at all?

No. Stop. Don't think that way. Dakar concentrated fiercely in the rest of her morning classes, as though she had built a box in her brain and could keep that thought inside. But at lunchtime, as she started toward the cafeteria, feeling hungry and a little shy about the way the whole middle school seemed to be buzzing with talk about the game, she couldn't keep the thought out of her head anymore. Mom and Dad were getting a divorce. Mom was never coming back.

"Are you that Tarzan girl's sister?" a boy asked

her. Dakar made a face at him. For a moment she wanted to stand up on the table and shout, "Yes, she's my sister, and her name is Jakarta." Another part of her wanted to hide under the table until lunch was over. She put her head down as she pushed the tray along its grooves. Don't think. Don't think.

"Africa child."

Dakar jerked her head up.

"Africa child, aren't you going to say hello?"

"Why—why are you here?" Dakar asked.

The cook gave her hips a self-satisfied pat. "You think Pharo would let me stay away with winter coming on? And miss this team he's been talking about? No, I was sitting in the sun, having such talks with my baby sister, but Pharo wouldn't leave me alone. He kept sending me postcards. 'You have to come home,' he kept writing. So here I am."

Dakar glanced behind her. She was holding up other people in line. How embarrassing. She rushed over to put her tray on the milk cart and trotted back to the kitchen. "Why did you decide to go, after all?"

"Got a call that my baby sister was sick," the cook said. "And I got to thinking about how you said that God was candlelight. And what about God showing up in the Bible as a dove? Birds fly, I thought. And that little Africa child flies. Aren't you ashamed to not be as brave as a child? Maybe there's a time to be anchored down and a time to fly."

The cook thought she was brave? Dakar shook her head. Not even biting on her thumb could keep away the tears in the corner of her eyes. "Why didn't you say good-bye?" she whispered.

The cook clicked her tongue softly. "Africa child, you've been all curled tight around your feelings, hiding them away," she said. "I can see you're starting to uncurl a little bit. That's good. Life is already a dry and weary land without hiding your true self away from the people who care about you."

Okay, she *had* been curled tight, Dakar thought, hunched over her tray at one of the back tables. Just like a water baby. But what happened if you uncurled? Your insides were all bare and unprotected. Those bare insides helped you be close to other people, but then what happened to the people you cared about? Hoodies got them. Or you had to leave them behind.

For the rest of the day she imagined herself

tucked inside a turtle shell, a nice, strong, safe shell. The only time she poked her head out was when Mr. Johnson asked her a question in math class. As Dakar opened her mouth to answer, Melanie turned around, and for the second time that day they were suddenly looking right at each other.

Had she made it up, Dakar wondered later, or did Melanie sign, "Are you okay?"

SIXTEEN

The snow had stopped by the time Dakar stood by the bus and watched the basketball team load its gear. She hugged Jakarta, not caring who saw. "Make a thousand points," she whispered.

Jakarta laughed. "Okay. Don't worry about shoveling snow or anything. It's not like we have a car to get out of our driveway."

When Dakar got home, the wind was starting. Even after she was inside, she could hear it slithering around the house, moaning at the cracks. She set to work cleaning everything she could think of, liking the solid feel of her hands in soapy water. In Africa they always had house workers. Everyone did—not just the *ferenji, mzungu, khawaaga* but middle-class African families, too. So she didn't really know much about cleaning, but it was kind of fun, and it made the time pass.

She ate cold cereal for supper, reading in between bites. Too bad Mom and Dad thought television was mind rot. Mostly she didn't miss having one, but tonight she could use the sound of another voice.

When she got to the end of the chapter she was on, she checked her watch. Jakarta would be warming up now. "Loose as a goose," she whispered, concentrating on Jakarta's arms, her legs, her arms. It was Jakarta's *mind* that had to stay the most loose. Dakar had seen Jen and Beth get nervous, once they finally got sent in, and miss shots they always made in practice.

At seven-thirty she went to the front door and poked her head outside. The game would be starting. Dakar concentrated on that moment when everything was possible, the two centers crouched, all the focus and energy sucked into the whirlpool created when the ref bent down to toss the ball in the air. "Go, Jakarta," she shouted. The air was fuzzy with snow.

"See, I'm fine," she said out loud. She shut the door and locked it. And for a long time she was. She didn't want to go upstairs without Jakarta, so she made a nest on the downstairs couch and curled up there with her books. It was only later, later when the wind just wouldn't stop howling and seemed to have grown scratching fingers, that she got scared. What if an escaped convict had gotten away from the nearest prison (wherever that was) and was scratching at the door, working his way inside? What if a snake was crawling up the shower drain? What if . . .

She dashed upstairs for supplies—two blankets, her pillow, books, and candles—and rushed back down slip-sliding her hand along the banister so she wouldn't tumble. In the living room she put her pillow over her head and tried to think. Melanie's cousin had said Jakarta was about to set a record. Even though she'd joined the team late, she was about to make more points than any girl in the whole, entire school, ever.

Jakarta would surely stay around then, especially if Mom and Dad were here to cheer her on and tell her how great she was doing. Don't give up. Don't give up, O ye of little faith. But what to do? She dug in the bookshelves until she found a book of Psalms. She closed her eyes, opened the book, and pointed her finger without looking. Psalm 137. "By the rivers of Babylon—there we sat down and there we wept when we remembered Zion. On the willows there we hung up our harps. For how could we sing the Lord's song in a foreign land?" Dad must feel that way living in Cottonwood—even if Dakar had never seen a moth that had a harp to hang up.

"Foo," she told the psalm. But it was zero help

in figuring out what to do. She felt foolish. In boarding school one of Dakar's roommates said she'd heard of someone who tried this and put his finger on "Judas went out and hanged himself." He shut the Bible, opened it again, and put his finger on "Go thou and do likewise."

She lit a candle. "Trust the universe," she chanted. "The universe is goodness all around you." Was that the same thing as saying, "The earth and the firmament are full of the glory of God"? People were always trying to find the words to wrap around the mysteries. "Trust the universe," she said again. She hated the sound of her out-loud voice in the empty living room. And the candle made scary shadows. She blew it out.

When the phone suddenly rang, her stomach lurched. Mom! A half second later she realized this was her chance. Pharo had told his mom, "You have to come home." It might be selfish, but she could do that, too. Who made Jakarta boss of how everything should be? Yes! she thought as she ran to pick it up.

"Dakar?" It was Dad's voice, faraway and faint. "How's it going?"

She wanted to say, "I'm scared. Really scared," but how could you say that to someone who would say, "It is a poor life in which there is no fear"? Had the kitchen door just moved? She watched it carefully. No. Must be the light in here.

"Dakar?"

"I'm okay," she said. "What are you doing?"

"We're staying in a house for the weekend, so I'm finally near a phone. The camps are bad. People are desperate for blankets. We've heard aid is getting to Guatemala City, but it's not reaching the camps, so two of us are off tomorrow to find out what we can about that."

Dakar felt a sudden tenderness curling up her throat. Dad always could be counted on to leap to the defense of anything that couldn't fight for itself.

She listened to him talk about the camps, and suddenly he said, "How are my resourceful girls? Is your mom back yet?"

"Please come home," she wanted to say. "I don't feel resourceful anymore." She said, "We're doing okay. Do you think most of the people you're trying to help will end up okay?"

After she hung up, she frowned at the telephone. Stupid universe—made the wrong one call. Well. She checked the clock. Jakarta would be home soon. It was already ten and the game should be over.

Something outside clunked against the side of the house, and Dakar inched to the window and tried to see out, her heart pounding like a loud, annoying song. All she could see was snow. Then the phone rang again.

This time it was Jakarta calling to say that the bus was stuck. "One of my teammates let me use her cell phone. Coach says there's probably white-out conditions wherever there are open fields between here and Cottonwood." The phone crackled for a moment. "He says it might be a danger-ous, slow-going trip. Don't wait up."

"D-dangerous?"

"Don't worry about me," Jakarta said impa-tiently. "Hang on a second." The phone went silent, and then Jakarta's voice came back on. "See. Coach just said we're not even going to try to drive home tonight. Lock all the doors and hop in bed, okay? I have a whole team to help figure out where we're going to sleep."

Dakar made herself a cup of cocoa as if filling up her stomach would help fill up the empty hole inside. Back in the living room she curled up with her cocoa and tried to read again. This time her mind kept buzzing every time she turned a page. What *were* those clunking sounds?

She dragged two chairs into the living room

and managed to drape her blanket so that it made a tent. There. Now she didn't have to look at the whole big living room. "I'm fine," she whispered. And Jakarta, who had a whole team to help her figure things out, would definitely be fine. She snaked her arm out of the tent, grabbed her lists and thoughts book, and wrote, "I wish I had a team."

1. Mom and Dad would be on my team.
2. The problem is that Dad is in Guatemala and Mom is on some North Dakota farm.
3. You live in the U.S. now, Dakar. Have you ever heard of such a thing as long-distance calls?
4. I've never made a long-distance call before.
5. That is so stupid. You are in sixth grade. Sixth graders know how to make long-distance calls.
6. But I don't.
7. Anyway, Aunt Lily doesn't have a phone.

She snaked her arm out, again, and reached around for her pillow. There. She was an elephant, rooting around for everything she needed, using the delicate tip of her trunk to feel things out. "Did you know an elephant's trunk has 150,000 muscles?" she wrote in her book.

With the second blanket wrapped around her and her head on the pillow, she closed her eyes and chanted softly to herself. "The universe is goodness all around me. Genesis, Exodus, Leviticus, Numbers, Deuteronomy." Think of something pleasant, some time when the four of them were together. She was back in Kenya sitting with Dad at their favorite camping place at Lake Naivasha. Perfect. She even had the tent.

Dad's arm was around her shoulders, and he was pointing to an impala that stared for a moment and then pronked away, making both of them laugh. That afternoon they'd all gone hiking in the lower gorge. It was a supaloaf time until she started to read the guide they'd picked up at the gate. "If you cross to the far side of the dam," it said, "beware! The deep pool at the head of the spring is guarded at times by a large black cobra!"

Then they were deep in the gorge, walking between walls so high that sometimes they could hardly see the sky. Jakarta was studying trails of eggs streaming out from the frogs they could see everywhere in the stream. Mom was pointing out a tall, glossy acacia tree she wanted to come back and paint. No one would pay attention when

Dakar showed them the place in the guide that said, "You need to keep an eye on the weather. When there is a torrential downpour in the hills and cliffs above, the water starts racing from here for ten kilometres down the Njorowa Gorge, sweeping all vegetation, gravel, and even huge boulders before it."

"Look," she'd told them. "Look at the clouds." But they wouldn't look. Sure enough, they'd barely climbed up the last steps out of the gorge when the first fat raindrops had pelted them. Why didn't anyone care about keeping this family all safe except for her? No wonder she had to worry.

Suddenly she was sick of it. She put her head on the pillow, tears leaking out of the corners of her eyes. No more quests. Enough.

After what seemed like hours and hours she had finally drifted off to sleep when a crash knocked her half awake. In her drowsiness she was sure she and Dad were on a camping trip, cautiously slipping from bush to bush, following the hippo trail. Dad pointed silently to the elephants about a hundred feet ahead, browsing in the trees. Every muscle in Dakar's body felt tense.

One of the elephants raised his head, ears fanned. He poked his trunk in the air and looked straight at Dakar. Out of the corner of her eye she saw the trackers lift their rifles to Position One.

Dad was touching her arm. She unfroze and stepped behind a tracker. Slowly they all started walking backward. The elephant trumpeted, an air-shivering sound. He took several steps forward, pawing the ground. He took another step.

Dakar couldn't breathe.

Then, in deadly silence, the elephant charged. Dakar was running, running backward. All she could think about was that she was going to trip. The elephant would be on them in perhaps six seconds when one of the trackers suddenly stopped, dropped to one knee, and fired over the elephant's head. *Pop, pop, pop, pop.*

Dakar screamed and opened her eyes. Wait. She was in North Dakota. But what was that crash? Cautiously she poked her head out of the tent. Even with the light on, the living room corners were silver, whispering shadows. The insides of Dakar's eyelids felt as if someone had just scrubbed them with a rough washcloth.

No! Dakar pulled her head back and started to pound the pillow with all her strength. Nooooo. She was just a kid. Maybe everybody did need for her not to need them, but it was just too,

too much. She grabbed the pen and started to scribble.

1. I'm TIRED of being brave and resourceful.
2. I'm tired of having Donbirra eyes and hiding what I'm thinking from everybody.
3. I'm don't WANT to be the hero of my own life anymore, no matter what Dad says.
4. I'm tired of being a princess and having to do impossible tasks. It is too HARD to keep the faith.
5. I want a T E A M. Team.
6. I give up. I give up. I GIVE UP.

SEVENTEEN

She woke up the next morning with the light still on and her fingers curled around the pen. Her eyes went right to the list. Don't think. Don't think. She crawled out of her tent and put on her coat and gloves.

Outside, she could see what the clunking and crashing had been all about. Branches. The snow must have been too heavy for them. She'd never seen a world turn white this way. She stomped down the sidewalk, amazed at the clear footprints her shoes left in the snow.

At Melanie's house long icicles hung from the eaves. Cool, Dakar thought, and laughed grimly at her own joke. She knocked on one of them with her glove, then shook it. It came off in her hand. She reached out and tapped it lightly on Melanie's window.

The curtains wiggled. Dakar couldn't see the expression on Melanie's face. At least she didn't see any purple on her hair yet. She held her breath. The face disappeared. A few seconds later the door opened.

"Melanie," Dakar said quickly. It was so weird the way her breath really did puff out when she talked. "I don't deserve for you to be my friend again because I know I was mean and rude. I'm only asking your help for one thing that I'm sure would help the Lady Wildcats out. One thing. A hard thing for me that would be easy for you, but by the way, you have to promise not to tell *anyone*."

Please, she thought. Please be interested in helping the Lady Wildcats to victory.

"And here." Dakar held out the icicle. "This is the sword of truth that you can impale me with if I'm not telling the total and absolute truth, and I'm not going to *stop* even one time."

"Kid-hey!" Melanie said, reaching for the icicle. "Get in here." Her eyes were zingy with excitement. "You mean, you're having a real, true secret adventure and you even *thought* about not asking me?"

"Actually," Dakar said, "I think it would work better if you came to my house."

On the way, light-headed with relief, she explained everything.

"Wow," Melanie said. "All right . . . it's coming to me. I can see this calls for an adventuresome secret plan. How big is this town where your aunt Lily lives?"

Inside the house Melanie grabbed the cordless telephone and a phone book. "In there," she said, waving at the tent.

"It's a good place to scheme," Dakar agreed. She felt like kissing Melanie's hand.

"First, we need to make sure it's the same area code."

Dakar looked over Melanie's shoulder. Next time she would know about area codes.

"Yep. Seven-oh-one," Melanie said. "Now I'm calling directory assistance."

"Aunt Lily doesn't have a phone," Dakar reminded her.

"Oh, right." Melanie hung up and started chewing on her thumbnail.

It was Melanie who came up with the idea of seeing if they could get the name of the local grocery store—"Everybody buys food," she said—and Dakar who suddenly said, "What about the post office?"

"Perfect!" Melanie started to dial again. "My grandma lives in a small town, and the postmaster knows everyone." After a few minutes of talking she said, "There! All you have to do is dial a one and then this number."

Dakar swallowed. "I don't think I can," she squeaked.

Melanie laughed. "Here. Fine. I'll do it. What's her last name again?"

The woman on duty at the post office turned out to be the daughter of the postmistress, filling in because her mother was sick. "I don't remember all the older people," she said, "but my mother would. Not an emergency, but very important, huh? When I get off work this evening, I'll go right over there, and we'll figure out something. If we can track her down, what should I say?"

"Uh, just a minute," Melanie said. She and Dakar had a whispered conference. Then Melanie said, "Please give Deborah the message that her daughters called. Say their dad was called away, and her daughters need her at home."

After Melanie hung up, they scrambled out of the tent and rolled around the floor, laughing and giving each other high fives. "I was great, huh?" Melanie said. "Want to come to my house until Jakarta gets back? I can show you how to make snow angels."

"Sure." Dakar could feel joy rippling across her chest like a jagged stream of lightning. "Just let me put this stuff away so Jakarta doesn't have a heart attack when she gets home."

□   □   □

The rest of Saturday flew by in a blur. That evening, as Dakar listened to Jakarta giving her all the details of the game, she couldn't keep from glancing at the window. Was that a car she heard? No. It was as bad as waiting for the Jeep in Maji. And as disappointing.

All Sunday she waited. Nothing. "I guess she's not coming," Dakar told Melanie on the phone.

"Well, she'd have to find someone to take care of her aunt. You didn't want to worry your mom, remember, so we said it wasn't an emergency."

"I guess." Dakar hung up, feeling numb. When had Africa turned into Babylon for Mom? It hadn't always been that way, had it? But at some point Mom must have hung her harp on the willow, alone and melancholy.

"I'm sending an e-mail to Dad," Jakarta called from downstairs. "Want me to tell him anything?"

"Yeah," Dakar called back. "Tell him to stay away from shaky buildings."

At least the Bear Lake game would help keep her mind off Mom. The cheerleaders had even come by the house and put up a big sign that said, GO, JAKARTA! TAKE US TO VICTORY.

"Isn't this too much pressure?" Dakar asked as she and Jakarta stood outside and looked at it. Was she just imagining things, or were cars slowing down? Would people driving by see the sign? "What if your shot's off or something?"

"Everyone's shot is off sometimes," Jakarta said. "Coach says to be patient and calm. There's nothing to do but have confidence and keep shooting."

Jakarta's shot was not off. Dakar could tell even in the warm-ups that she was hitting. "How tough is this Wildcat team, really?" a man said behind her. "Think they can finally beat those Bear Lake kids?"

"Don't know," another man answered. "Bear Lake's football team just slaughtered us. Of course, the football team this year is cream . . . cream *puffs*."

"Those Bear Lake farm kids build muscles baling hay," the first man said. "Our kids are softies compared to farm kids. They can't compete."

Dakar looked around. She'd never seen the gym this packed. How could Jakarta hear anything? How could she be calm enough to move around the top of the key, making basket after basket?

"That girl can shoot," the man behind her said.

Ha. She's never even baled hay, either, Dakar thought.

The men talked through the whole game. Once

when the ref whistled a foul on Jen, one of them shouted, "That's all right. It was a good foul. Next time you foul, though, take her *out*."

Dakar was glad Dad wasn't here to hear that. "Let's not take this wildcat thing quite that seriously," she muttered.

At halftime the announcer talked about how Jakarta now had 469 season points, close to a school record. Some kids in front stood up and started to cheer.

"History in the making!" the loud guy behind Dakar shouted.

"At this rate," the other guy said, "she'll break the state record. Maybe even next year."

Then everyone was hollering. But Jakarta just stood there with fierce eyes, not looking the least bit flustered.

Dakar felt so bursting with pride that even her feet were warm when she walked home in the snow. The minute she saw the house, she knew instantly that something was different. What was it? Was the house trying to tell her its name? Oh! Of course. Thistle gray smoke drifting out of the chimney. Dakar started to run.

"Mom?" she shouted as she shoved the door open.

The house smelled of wood smoke and roasting corn. Mom and a little gnome woman with wispy white hair were sitting by the fireplace, both looking a bit frail. Mom jumped up and held out her arms. Her face was full of puzzlement and pain, and as they stared at each other, Dakar could feel all the things she'd been squashing for so long rushing up and into her own eyes. She wished she could make herself be stronger for Mom. Pale, blank eggshell eyes weren't pretty, but at least they were calm and expressionless.

"Come here," Mom said, and Dakar ran to her. Okay. Crying wasn't the end of the world. "How are you?" Mom said finally. "How's Jakarta?"

"She's so great. You missed the best game!"

"What's this about your dad?"

"I . . ." Dakar opened her mouth. She closed it again.

"He hasn't been here for some time, has he?" Mom said faintly.

Dakar shut her eyes. Mom had always had that sense about those things. "He's in Guatemala," she said unhappily. Something clunked at the front door. Jakarta must be home.

"Guatemala." Mom shivered slightly. "No, I don't think so."

"Yes . . ." Dakar stopped. The door opened. The smell of incense and sweat swept in.

FROM DAKAR'S BOOK
OF LISTS AND THOUGHTS

Synchronicity

Dad was in line to buy a ticket to Guatemala City when he suddenly heard the woman in back of him say "*Dakar.*" He turned around but she was just talking to a friend beside her. Then she said, "I'm sure he's doing good things in Dakar, but . . . don't you think some people find it easier to love the whole world than the people right beside them?" Next thing Dad knew, he was at the counter asking about flights to Minneapolis.

Mom didn't get my message until Sunday morning, and then Aunt Lily wanted to come, too. So they had to wait for Monday morning to get Aunt Lily's medication. So now everybody is here—even Aunt Lily. But how maddening! They made me come up to bed and they're still talking. What they don't know is that I'm sitting at the top of the stairs trying to hear.

I thought Mom would be happy to see Dad, but after he explained what happened, she stared at him as if she were seeing a tree fungus. "It's so great to be home," he said. Mom looked like a water buffalo about to charge. "Whoa," he said, backing up. He laughed but a bit nervously.

Now Dad is shouting. "Look!" he's saying. "I assumed they'd tell you when you called. Besides, they were fine, weren't they? I was living three continents away from my parents when I was Jakarta's age."

Jakarta is shouting, too. "Look!" she's saying. "We made it, didn't we? We were fine, weren't we? We were resourceful, just like little kids in East Africa—and Guatemala, I'm sure."

I hope they're all *looking*. Whenever this family is back together, why does everyone have to be mad?

EIGHTEEN

Dakar woke up to noises—voices below, someone laughing, the scrape of a shovel outside. She got dressed as quickly as she could and rushed downstairs. At the stove Aunt Lily was perched on a stool, sculpting paper-thin pancakes. First she drizzled batter onto the pan in a circle. A few minutes later, she loosened the edges of the pancake with deft fingers and flipped it. After a moment, she scooped it onto a plate. "Sit down," she told Dakar. "Uf-dah, you're skinny, my dear. You need to eat." On the table three jars of homemade jelly sat like jewels: translucent coral, pale green, sumptuous purple.

"How are you feeling?" Dakar asked.

Aunt Lily gave her a gleeful smile. "I got up and checked the obituaries, and I wasn't in there, so I know it's going to be a great day."

Dakar put her arms around Mom, soaking in the smells of the kitchen, the spattering sound of water dripping, the *scrape, scrape* from outside the window that must be Dad shoveling snow.

"I raked all the leaves," she said shyly. "I wish you could have seen how glorious the yard looked. It would have made you feel all picket-fency."

Mom's shoulders felt thin. She was the one who needed pancakes.

"Ah, what we'll have to look at in the spring!" she said. "Please put the butter on, Dakar."

"And Jakarta, Mom. You should see her. She has an away game Wednesday, but she better not break the record there because I want to see her break it, and so does everybody else."

"Oh, you know it!" Aunt Lily said. "That girl had better wait."

"Mom?" Dakar paused. She wanted to say, "Are you still mad at Dad?" But that would break the spell of the jeweled kitchen morning.

She made three pancakes slithery with butter—with a different jelly on each one—and didn't even care that butter dripped down her chin.

When Jakarta came downstairs, yawning, Dakar told her, "I'm going to stop by Melanie's house on the way to school." She didn't bother to say, "Are you coming?" Whatever Jakarta thought, Melanie was on her team.

Jakarta followed Dakar up the sidewalk, without saying a word. Melanie came bouncing out.

Stopped. "I haven't touched an onion since that night, you know," she finally said to Jakarta.

"We're even," Jakarta said. "I never touched snow before this week."

Dakar could see from their expressions that that was that.

After Jakarta had turned toward the high school door, the girl with purple hair ran up to them. "Do you think Jakarta would teach me how to do a layup with my left hand?" she asked breathlessly.

"Probably," Dakar said. Imagine. Someone with purple hair wanted to be a better basketball player.

When Melanie introduced them, Dakar reached out and gravely shook the girl's hand, the way she'd been taught to do in Africa. Her name was Andrea, and she didn't look scary anymore. And her hair was fine.

All week Dakar felt special. Kids she didn't even know said "hey" to her. At lunch she sat with Andrea and her friends. When they swapped food, she gleefully handed over Aunt Lily's homemade cookies, remembering lunchtime trades at the student center by the little round cafeteria in Nairobi—Indian kids with dried mango strips, Taiwanese kids with metal tins of rice and pork,

Ethiopian kids with *wat* and *injera*. Dakar had been too shy there. Now she traded the homemade cookies for a cruddy granola bar just because it made her feel so un-*ferenji*, *-mzungu*, *-khawaaga* to be trading.

Wednesday afternoon they all went to Melanie's house and made little maroon-and-gray pompoms. I'm . . . *quivering* with joy, Dakar thought. She had actual friends, friends Jakarta didn't even know. And next Monday night Jakarta and her team were going to dazzle up and down the court in the last game of the season, the one that would get them into regionals. The Wildcats were going to win easily—everyone said it. Best of all, Jakarta was going to set a school record, and her name would go forever on the wall o' jocks. Jakarta would be a Wildcat superstar. And she, Dakar thought, hugging herself, would be the sister of a superstar.

"Hey," Melanie said, "will you tell them the story of Donbirra?"

Dakar opened her mouth, then paused, trying to think through what she'd been about to say. Would she betray her memories if she made them into stories? If she didn't start talking about them, though, Jakarta was right. Soon they'd be gone. She took a deep breath and put her best storytelling voice on.

"I'll do something better," she said. "I'll tell you true stories of things that happened to me in Africa."

That afternoon she ran home, slipping and sliding on the shoveled sidewalks. Dad couldn't stay outside and shovel all day. How would things be now? Cautiously, she opened the door. She could hear voices, and they weren't hollering. Someone had been baking cinnamon bread. She closed the door quietly behind her and tiptoed toward the voices.

". . . could hear the clank of pots and pans," Dad was saying as she peeked into the living room. "It was the mules arriving from one direction. Meanwhile, I heard shouts from another direction as the group that had gone looking for our supper came back with the gazelle they had shot." It was one of his favorite true stories about a time when he and a research team had gone out from Maji to gather information in the remote mountains. Aunt Lily was sitting on the couch with a blanket over her knees. She looked up with a smile and waved Dakar in. Dakar grinned. Dad must be okay, then— contrite, absolved, forgiven.

She curled up beside Aunt Lily. This was one story she knew almost by heart. Dad was about to say, "I was suddenly aware of another sound: a low, intense buzzing. 'Bees!' I yelled as the air filled with furious brown clouds of them." Aunt Lily reached out and patted her. Dakar felt like a cat, with Dad's story tickling her ears and chin.

The men dived for cover in the brush. The mules bucked in all directions, pots and pans ringing madly, seeming to make the bees even more angry. Dad, in the middle of the biggest cloud, slapped at his neck and waved his arms around as he ran. Swiftly, he swept off the few bees still clinging to his skin. He could count nineteen welts from his neck up. His face was getting puffy.

Hungry and sore, they huddled in the brush for hours. Finally, the Amhara cook managed to sneak past the bees and get mosquito nets for everyone. The next day most of the group went off, ferried across the river by tall Teshena warriors in their dugout canoes. Dad, who had volunteered to stay behind with the cook, watched how the men paddled furiously to the middle of the river to catch the current, then maneuvered into an eddy with a back current that brought the canoes in a circle to the other shore. When the others were gone, the cook showed Dad how to make *kita*, unleavened journey bread, and the two of them sat trading stories, eating the bread, and drinking strong tea.

Early the next morning the cook, who knew some Teshena, woke Dad to say that he had overheard drunken boasts from the Teshena warriors. "They will first kill us and steal the mules. They will kill the others when they have brought them back over the river."

Dad wasn't sure what to think. Was this just typical Amhara mistrust of other ethnic groups? But it was true that the village was eerily still, no women calling to each other as they pounded grain, no smell of cook fires, no children playing. Unfortunately, there were no other places where the river was safe to cross. And the research team had to be ferried back to the side Dad was on in order to get home. Quietly the cook and Dad packed up. Then they blew air into the air mattresses and tied them in a double layer. When the research team returned, Dad shouted the news across the river and then paddled his makeshift raft to the middle, trying to catch the current the way he'd seen the men in the canoes do. He had just found the current when he heard shouts. Rising slowly out of the brown water were the eyes of a crocodile. Someone shot a rifle, and the eyes disappeared.

Dakar shivered. What a trip that was. Dad got

everyone safely across, and the village stayed silent, so silent he wondered if anyone was even there, if the cook had somehow misunderstood what was happening. He never did find out. But as they began the trip back, they gradually discovered the mules had saddle sores and couldn't carry the gear back up Maji Mountain. Dad and a Maji police-man volunteered to climb for help. So they set off with no food to stave off their hunger except a lit-tle roasted grain the policeman had along. At dusk they ran into a snarling cheetah. Luckily, when the policeman cocked his pistol, the cheetah leaped off into the brush.

She'd always liked the end, when Dad got home in the middle of the night and shook Mom awake. "What are you doing here?" Mom said. He told her to wake him at dawn so he could go back to rescue the others with the Jeep. Dakar had never before thought to wonder what Mom felt as she shone her flashlight up into Dad's puffy, bee-stung face.

"Merciful heavens," Aunt Lily said. "You remind me of my late husband. Otis used to say, 'Don't take needless risks, but do take interesting ones.' "

"Great-Uncle Otis was very different from Grandpa, wasn't he?" Dakar asked.

"Yes," Aunt Lily said. "Otis was a different breed

of fish altogether. Charles believed one of life's greatest blessings was to die in the same place you were born. Otis had no roots to speak of. But you know, they had a lot in common. Charles could see beauty in rippling prairie greasy grass under the moon. Otis could see the beauty in just the right tuck of the chin—or in a graceful fall. They both had the gift of doing one thing at a time."

Mom had that gift, Dakar thought. Jakarta, too. She herself would have liked to have it, but she was more like Dad. Restless. With a start she realized that Aunt Lily was saying something else. "On one of our visits home I heard the two of them philosophizing out by the barn. I heard Charles say life wasn't a matter of fearlessness but of practicing courage. Otis said he made it a point to make friends with one of his fears every day. 'Life is terrifying,' he said. 'Terrifying—and wonderful.' "

Dad stood up.

"Terrifying and wonderful," Dakar said to herself. It sounded like a good thing to hang on to. She hoped she could remember it long enough to write it down.

She was getting up to go upstairs and find her lists and thoughts book when Aunt Lily reached over and grabbed her hand and pressed it to her own heart for a moment.

"Can you feel the happiness pumping?" Aunt Lily asked. "I thought you would stay in Africa forever and I'd never get to meet you. I thought I would never see any of my family again."

FROM DAKAR'S BOOK
OF LISTS AND THOUGHTS

I sat with Aunt Lily tonight while Mom and Dad went to get groceries. I asked her to tell me the story of the Great Cadona. She said exactly what Mom already had told me.

Do you believe in magic? I asked her. She told me you can't travel with a circus and not see a good many astounding things. Most are frauds. Some aren't.

But do you believe we can change the way things are going to turn out? I asked. She said, Of course we can. Courage changes things, doesn't it? Kindness changes things. She said, Don't you think practicing courage and kindness and things like that sends little magic slivers into the world?

But if the Great Cadona was watching over Great-Uncle Otis, I said, why did he fall? I was afraid I'd gone too far. But she didn't seem to mind. Yes, there's that, she said. That and the fact that we all die of something sooner or later.

She told me about casting. Casting is the invisible demon of the circus tent, she said. In one part of an instant the mind just seems to let go. And then you can't hold on any longer. One time six people fell in the same month after years of no accidents.

Then how can people say Trust God? I asked her. Trust the universe?

Well, she said, they say the universe is at least a hundred million years old, and I'm sure it has more tricks and riddles up its sleeves than I'll understand. But Otis trusted, and I had to trust, or I would have lived my whole life with Otis in a cloud of fear.

Besides, she said, what if I hadn't trusted? Otis would still have fallen. Rose would still have died of cancer. Iris would still have flown away and crashed. But I would have been busy fretting and missed all the lovely moments.

Because life is wonderful? I said.

That's right, she said. Terrifying and wonderful.

NINETEEN

Thursday night Mom and Aunt Lily sat with their cups of coffee, their heads bent over a crossword puzzle. "Isn't *burgundy* a wine color?" Aunt Lily asked.

"*Bordeaux* is, too," Mom said. "And it has the same number of letters."

Dakar looked around, wishing she could hang on to this moment. Jakarta was doing homework. Only Dad was pacing, looking howlingly restless.

As if Mom had read Dakar's mind, she suddenly said, "I don't think winter's so bad. After all, we have central heat and fluffy things to wear when we're outside." She told Aunt Lily, "In Egypt the apartment wasn't heated. I never got warm except when I was taking hot baths."

Dakar nodded. She could remember sleeping with her head under the covers and trying to tuck them in all around so no air could get in.

"Remember the sky?" Dad asked somberly. "It was dark gray all the time. Just like here this week. Anyone would have to be crazy to want to live through a North Dakota winter."

"It won't be this gray often," Aunt Lily said. "They say the clouds keep the temperature up."

Dad leaned over and laid another log on the fire. "So I can be cheerful and freezing or warm and depressed?" He looked up, dusting off his hands, and caught Dakar watching him. "What?"

"You want to go back to Kenya, don't you?"

Dad stepped toward the table. In the firelight his reddish beard looked a little like a burning bush. "Well, I'm trying," he said impatiently. "But all this gray. I feel as if I'm staring upward from the bottom of a deep river." His voice got even more impatient. "In the middle of the sweaty action—digging latrines or whatever—you're exhausted, sometimes scared, but you're not fretting about some trivial thing. The minute you go home, the hardship is gone, but so are the friendships and the feelings that you're doing something powerful."

Mom sighed. "You're thinking about it, aren't you? You're thinking that we promised never to say no to an adventure. I—" She choked and looked down.

The room was quiet except for a log hissing in the fireplace.

Then Aunt Lily patted Dad's hand. "Sometimes some people need to be in a garden for a while," she said. "A nice, sheltered, sunny spot out of the wind. Sometimes, instead of soaring, they need to put down roots and be carrots."

"I suppose," Dad said doubtfully. "What do you think we should do, Dakar?"

Dakar swallowed and glanced away, so she wouldn't see the expression in his eyes. *I cannot choose, I cannot choose.* Why did it have to be that no matter where she lived, she was always going to be missing something or someone?

Mom was still staring at her knees, and Dakar wanted to run over and hug her. When Mom looked up, though, it was Aunt Lily she looked at. *Maybe Mom needs mothering, too*, Jakarta had said. But what about the jacaranda trees? What about hearing lovely African words again? But—but . . .

"I think we should stay," Dakar said.

"Jakarta?"

Jakarta looked up. Dakar's stomach clenched and unclenched like a fist. *I cannot choose.*

"I don't know," Jakarta said. From the sound of her voice anyone would have guessed they were discussing the price of turnips. She seemed to be the only calm one in the room. As everyone looked at her, she slowly put down her pen and snapped her book shut. "Let me think about it. I'm going to bed now. We play the Storm on Monday, and they're famous for pounding guards. I'm getting plenty of rest between now and then."

"That's right," Dad said. "The record."

"It isn't about individual honors. It's about getting to state. We're going in there as a team." Jakarta shot Dad a defiant look as she went out.

The next day it was a relief to get to school. At lunch Dakar told stories about her favorite places to eat in Nairobi: the Indian restaurant where they ate tandoori chicken washed down with "a Stoney," the restaurant where you could order ostrich egg omelets, and the Village Market, which really wasn't a market at all, Dakar explained, but a mall with trendy little shops, where Mom let Dakar and Jakarta buy their own suppers on busy evenings.

They'd researched the best combinations: an order of nuggets, shared, for 140 shillings and two orders of onion rings (30 shillings each) from Southern Fried Chicken. Chips—"what you'd call french fries"—from Hot 'n Not. For their last 110 shillings, they would get something to drink and candy floss from Slush. If they were celebrating something special or feeling rich, they'd have an extra dessert at Arlecchino Italian Ice Cream, not just *cioccolato, vaniglia,* or *granita de fragola*—straw-berry—but *crema alluovo* with a rich eggnog taste, or tart, tangy mango, guava, pineapple, or passion fruit. Every Friday, Village Market had a big Maasai open-air market where you could bargain for thousands of things piled out on straw mats: drums, Samburu beads, little carved half hippos, Kamba three-legged stools—

Andrea interrupted. "For cool," she said. "I thought the coolest thing about you was that you were Jakarta's sister. But now I see you're cool for yourself. Too bad I can't listen to you all day and not go to class."

"Really?" Dakar blushed. "I thought you didn't like me."

"Oh." Andrea tugged thoughtfully at a blond wisp of hair that stuck out from the purple at the nape of her neck. "We thought you didn't like us."

After school Melanie groaned and rolled her eyes when Dakar told her what Dad had asked. Then she twisted the bottom of her shirt into a knot, staring off into space. "If Jakarta gets the record, don't you think she'll want to stay?" she said finally.

"I think so. I heard someone say that by next year she'll probably set a new state record. Don't you think she'll wanna start working toward that?"

Melanie chewed a fingernail. "Probably. And then your dad will stay, too?"

"That's the feeling I got last night."

"You know what this calls for, don't you?" Melanie whispered.

"What?" Dakar looked at Melanie, puzzled.

Suddenly they both said together, "The magic place."

They ran all the way there. Dakar couldn't get her breath because she couldn't stop laughing. But they didn't stop running when they got to the magic place. They ran in circles in the melting snow, shouting, "Monkey toe, camel bones, petals of lotus, three. Elephant tusk. Hair of dog. Bark of sycamore tree. Wing of eel. Tooth of snail. Golden lion's mane. Giraffe's eyelash. Murmur of bat. Three silver birds flying home in the rain."

Dakar's head felt light and zingy. This kind of magic making was fun.

"I just have this feeling that everything's going to work out," Melanie said.

Dakar hugged her. True friendship must be another one of those things that sent magic slivers into the world. "Me, too," she said.

Nothing could shake her feeling. Jakarta spent almost the entire weekend in the gym. Sunday afternoon Mom drove Aunt Lily and Dakar over to the school so they could watch Jakarta practice. "You've got to see how many threes she can make when no one's guarding her," Dakar told them.

On Monday morning Dakar visited the wall o' jocks, just for good luck. "Don't feel bad," she felt like saying to Promise Johnson. "Your record stood for ten years. They'll probably keep your name up there somewhere."

"It'll be okay. It'll be okay," she found herself whispering all through the day.

Monday night she offered to do the dishes to make the time go faster. When she was finished, she did a little two-step into the living room, feeling a jittery exhilaration, exactly as if she were the one who was headed for glory. "Hey," she said, "I think it's time. We should go."

Dad was cleaning ashes out of the fireplace. He sat back on his heels. "So early?"

Aunt Lily put her pen down with a flourish. "Last game of the season. The gym will be jam-packed. Dakar, will you get my cane from the hallway?"

"Coming?" Mom asked Dad, almost casually.

"I'm tempted." He smiled. "But I think I'll say no. I'd rather encourage mending and building in my children than crushing and winning."

"Your daughter is quite a girl," Aunt Lily said. "Was she always athletic?"

"Always," Dad said. "When we couldn't find her in Maji, we'd look in the schoolyard and she'd be kicking the soccer ball around with the older schoolboys."

"She certainly is a natural at basketball, like my mother," Aunt Lily said.

"The thing that stands out most in my memory," Mom said, "is that if she ever got a challenge in front of her, she went after it tooth and nail. I suppose it's genetic. Naneh, Jakarta's birth mother, was determined to get out of her own sheltered upbringing. She talked her parents into letting her be an aide in the school because the headmaster was a friend of the family."

"Yes," Dad said dryly. "Naneh came to Indonesia because she wanted to do something for people and not simply be a pampered Persian princess. Her daughter just wants to play basketball."

Mom ignored him. "She once told me a story about her father's mother. Apparently Naneh's grandmother was from a wealthy but a village family, and after her son married into a sophisticated city family, he commanded his mother to learn to read so she wouldn't appear so provincial. One day he visited her, and she told him, 'Son, you commanded me to go to school. I didn't want to, but I did your bidding, and I have learned to read. Now, my son, I must tell you that if you command me to quit my school, I will not.' "

Good, Dakar thought. Jakarta had Strong Woman Genes from at least her great-grandmother on. She'd need them tonight. Everyone said the Storm was a tough, gritty team.

Dad stood up and walked over to the table. "Jakarta has a brilliant mind, too." His voice sounded frustrated and a little sad. "I always thought she'd find a way to wipe out malaria or something. Did you know that somewhere in the world a child dies of malaria every twelve seconds?"

Aunt Lily motioned to Dad, who helped her push back her chair. "I know what you mean," she said. "After Otis was killed, Iris said to me, 'Wouldn't you feel better if he had at least died doing something useful?' And I remembered the time Otis once told me that when he went to meet his Maker, his only hope would be to say he'd been an artist, creating sculptures in the air."

Dakar had a sudden image of what Great-Uncle Otis must have looked like, turning quadruple somersaults, making air sculptures with his tightly tucked knees.

"On the other hand," Aunt Lily said, using Dad's arm to help her stand up, "in confirmation class in a little Lutheran church long ago, on an evening when we had *lefse* with gooseberry sauce, the pastor had Iris and me memorize what one of the Church Fathers wrote: 'The glory of God is man fully alive.' "

"We'd better go," Mom said. She sounded edgy. "Or we won't get any seats at all."

Suddenly Aunt Lily's finger was on Dad's chest like a pin popping a balloon. "Jakarta might not be saving any lives or changing the world," she said. "But when she plays, she creates something beautiful."

In the stunned silence Dakar could tell from their expressions they both wanted to say more. Neither one did.

Finally Aunt Lily reached for her cane. "Merciful heavens," she said crisply, "let's not be late to see Jakarta set the school record."

They were almost out the door before Dad was there, pulling on his coat. "You're right," he said. Aunt Lily gave him a sharp look, and he laughed. "If we wait any longer," he said, putting his arm around her, "we might not get a seat."

TWENTY

The gym was rocking with noise by the time they got there. Dakar stepped through the door and stared up at the packed seats. The back-flipping cheerleader was doing her flips down the length of the gym. The high school band was playing. Some kids had painted their faces maroon-and-gray and were standing at the edge of the court with their arms around one another, shouting and doing high kicks. Dakar spotted Andrea's purple hair. If Mom and Dad weren't here, Dakar would be with the others, locked in the middle of a human chain. Her heart felt as big as all Africa.

"Where should we sit?" Mom was shouting.

"I don't know." Dakar looked helplessly around. They should have left even earlier. The gym was already so full. And Aunt Lily shouldn't be climbing too many steps.

"Hey!" It was Pharo, standing up, waving. "Seats over here."

Dad started in that direction, and Dakar let Aunt Lily and Mom go next. She wanted to sit at the end where she could go outside for a few minutes if it got too tense. They'd almost reached Pharo when she realized his mother was sitting beside him in a bright red coat, waving a little maroon-and-gray flag.

"Are you having a hallelujah moment?" Dakar called to her.

"I am," she called back. "Your sister has this whole town cheering together for something. And that's a hallelujah thing."

Dakar loved watching Pharo introduce Mom and Dad and Aunt Lily to his mother. "You have lived in Africa," the cook said, shaking her head. "Now there is a firmament that's full of the glory of God."

"Yes, these three have been out changing the world," Aunt Lily said loudly, settling beside her. "But sometimes people get weary."

"Doesn't the Good Book say not to be weary of well-doing?" the cook asked tartly.

"It does," Aunt Lily said, just as tartly. "But another wise writer says those who make up their minds to go and see the world must needs find it a weary journey. Some of us are going to do crossword puzzles and make quilts and soup, and when spring comes, we need someone to show us how to plant a garden in this soil."

The cook settled back and nodded. "I'll help you put in the peas and beans if you folks will tell me all about Africa while we hoe."

Cartwheels of sound suddenly rippled along the crowd, and people started leaping to their feet. The basketball team must be coming in. Dakar thought, as she jumped up, that Aunt Lily and the cook would be perfect friends. She could imagine the two of them—no, all five of them—Mom, Aunt Lily, Jakarta, the cook, and Dakar, standing in a tight, warm circle, planting beans. What about Dad? She sneaked a look at him, and he smiled and crossed his eyes at her.

The roar in the gym was dizzying. Dakar listened to the announcer's voice booming above it, and then the band started in on the school song. When the cheerleaders were introduced, they made a pyramid and flung the little pompoms into the stands. Aunt Lily caught one. She waved it wildly when the announcer called Jakarta's name and it was Jakarta's turn to run through the circle of paper and out into the middle of the floor. Jakarta had by far the loudest cheers. Even though Dakar had been so sure everything was going to be fine, she could feel nervousness rippling under her skin.

Within minutes she knew Jakarta must be nervous, too. Almost before anyone knew what was happening, the Storm had leaped out to a ten-point lead. Their tall center beat out the Wildcat center on the opening jump, and the Storm forward who drove in was fouled as she made her basket. She made the free throw, and that was three points right there. At the other end Jakarta shot a trey, but the ball rolled off the rim. "Two rolls and no coffee," the announcer said as the other team got the rebound and turned the possession into another two points.

Before you could blink, Dakar thought, the Wildcats had suddenly fallen apart, making only one basket to the Storm's six. "It's coming down around us like Jericho," the cook murmured.

"Come on, Wildcats!" Dakar screamed. Her throat felt scratchy with longing. She looked at Dad. He had a faraway expression on his face. What was he thinking? Would it make him feel better to see the Wildcats lose?

Jakarta didn't let the team unravel. When the coach gestured to call time-out—his voice drowned in the noise—Jakarta instantly made the T with her hands. Pharo tapped Dakar's shoulder. When she looked up, he said, "Jakarta knows what's up. She's coming out of this huddle supaloafed."

Dakar laughed. "She taught you that word?"

"The Storm point guard is on her like skin. That's the problem."

He was right, Dakar saw as the play started again. Jakarta couldn't seem to get a clear and open shot. But after she had forced a couple—and missed—she seemed to shake herself and settle down. By the end of the first quarter she had only two points, but she also had a bunch of assists. Most important, Pharo pointed out, the Wildcats were eating into the Storm's lead.

By the half the Wildcats were down by only three. While the team trotted out of the gym, carried by waves of sound, Coach Svedborg looked as if he might explode. "Uh-oh. Lecture time," Pharo said. Jakarta had her head down. When she got to where they were sitting, she glanced up and gave Pharo a half-smile. But it was Dad her eyes locked on to for one long, slow moment. Then she was gone.

They could still win, Dakar thought as she walked back toward the concession window to buy popcorn for Aunt Lily. Was there still a chance Jakarta could get her record? She tried to remember how many points Jakarta had made before in her good halves. The Storm's guards were definitely holding her down.

A boy from the middle school jostled her. "What's happening to Tarzan?" he asked.

"Yeah," the guy beside him said. "I thought she was supposed to be so great. The Storm is sweeping her into the gully."

Dakar's feet felt frozen to the floor.

"Aah," the first guy said. "She used to be great. But it's clutch time now."

Suddenly someone was reaching around Dakar and thumping the guy's shoulder. Dakar pulled back, startled. "Don't be such a nimwit," Melanie screeched at the boy. "Jakarta isn't clutching. She has nerves of obsidian. You—you nimrod."

"Whatever," one of the boys muttered. They walked on.

"What a dolt," Melanie said to Dakar.

"Yeah . . ." Dakar could feel a smile just swallowing up her face. "What a scarab beetle."

When they were done laughing, Dakar asked, "Do you want to meet my great-aunt Lily? She's in there waving one of our pompoms."

"Sure. I'll come sit with you." Melanie paused. "No, I gotta sit with my family because everyone's here. Even my cousin. But can I come over to meet her tomorrow? I'll stand with you right now while you get your stuff, and we'll concentrate on sending good thoughts to Jakarta." Melanie closed her eyes and chanted softly, "Be a river, Jakarta."

"Yeah, come over tomorrow," Dakar said. "I want you to meet Aunt Lily, and I want to show you my room. Be a river, Jakarta. Be a river."

The Storm started shooting layups with four minutes ticking down in halftime, but the Wildcats didn't come out until just before the whistle blew. "Big-time lecture," Pharo said knowingly. Whether it was the big-time lecture or Melanie's chant, something must have worked. Emily set a pick, and Jakarta hit a three, first thing. The whole team seemed to loosen their shoulders. Then, in minutes, everyone was on fire. But Jakarta was on superfire. Up. Swish. Up. Swish.

The crowd was on its feet. The crowd was with her. "Tarzan," they chanted as she took the ball down the court. "Tarzan. Tarzan."

"Why do they call her that?" Dad shouted to Dakar.

"I'll tell you after," she shouted back.

Ten points for Jakarta. Fourteen points. Seventeen. The Wildcats were now dominating. The

Storm coach called time-out, and the girl who was supposed to be guarding Jakarta kicked her home bench in frustration. Only ten points from the record, the announcer boomed. Across the gym Dakar saw Melanie doing a victory dance. That must be Melanie's cousin with his fists in the air.

As the fourth quarter started, Dakar doubted that anyone was worrying about who would win the game. Unless the Wildcats suddenly collapsed, they were going to regionals. "Record," some people started to chant. "Record, record." And Jakarta kept knocking down baskets. The Storm players were doing their best to sandwich her in a double team. They were just as determined, Dakar saw, to say, "I guarded the best scorer in the whole state and kept her from running away with the game."

The clock was ticking down. The gym was writhing with noise. Dakar's ears pounded, and she felt as if she were caught up in the middle of the hissing ocean. Suddenly, above it all, she heard Coach Svedborg screaming, "Take time out." Emily, who had the ball, signaled. For a second the Wildcats were milling, huddling, and then a whole new team was out on the floor—all except Jakarta.

"What's happening?" Dakar shouted to Pharo.

"Only garbage minutes left. Coach is putting in the kids who never get to play. The Storm will never catch us now."

"What about Jakarta?" Even before he answered, Dakar knew. Nobody else had anything at stake. But Jakarta—Jakarta could get the record. This was her last chance. Last minutes of the last game of the regular season. Dakar chewed her thumbnail anxiously, glancing across the gym to see if Melanie was doing the same.

The Wildcats took the ball on the side. Dakar stared at Jakarta, willing her to run, to leap. Those legs must still be strong—Africa legs. Runner legs. Her arms couldn't be tired yet. Be a river. Ball in to Jakarta. Jakarta dodged, and one of the inexperienced girls, someone whose name Dakar didn't know because she'd never seen her in a game before, set a good pick. Jakarta made a jump shot, over the defender's head. Swish.

"Two more to tie," someone screamed out.

Two more. Two more points. The game seconds were clicking down. "Foul them," Coach Svedborg yelled. His face was redder than ever. Someone did. The Storm player made both shots. Now. Wildcat ball. Fifteen seconds left.

Dakar was trembling. She felt connected to

every single person in this gym—yes, even the Storm. They all were part of this moment together. They all would remember it for a long, long time.

Okay, okay. Ball in. Crisp. Bounce pass. Right to Jakarta's willing hands. Dakar felt her heart floating, bursting. Jakarta was thundering down the court. Jakarta was a river, an antelope, a gazelle. The other team couldn't stop her. Yes! Yes! Hallelujah glory. They couldn't shut Jakarta down. "Tarzan," the crowd screamed. "Tarzan." Two points to tie the record. Three points for a brand-new record—not half Promise Johnson's—all Jakarta.

"Shoot a three," Dakar screamed. "A three."

In the last split second she saw it. Saw it as if she were a camera, catching one fluid motion and freezing it into stillness. Saw Sharyn—the blond girl from that day in practice. Knew. Exactly. What. Was. Going. To. Happen.

And it did.

Jakarta dished. Sharyn arched up. Released. The ball kissed the glass—and went in. *Blaaaaaaaap.* The end-of-game buzzer blared.

For a moment there was a shocked silence. Then the fans were pouring onto the floor. "Going to regionals," someone behind Dakar shouted.

"And on to state," someone else shouted back.

Dakar stood still, staring down at Jakarta.

The fans were pushing around the players, hugging, laughing.

Jakarta wasn't looking at them, though. She was looking at the coach, and his face was angry, his mouth wide open. Even from here Dakar could read the words. *"Why didn't you take the shot?"*

TWENTY-ONE

In the pandemonium Dakar lost everyone else. That was okay, she thought as she walked slowly across the parking lot filled with swirls of people. She felt dazed. Let Dad get Aunt Lily and Mom out of there and safely home. She didn't want to talk to anyone.

As she was swept along, she caught sight of Melanie for a moment, a few cars away. "Are you okay?" Melanie signed.

True friend Melanie. "Fine," Dakar signed back. Not fancy fine, she thought. But fine.

As she got herself free of the people and started walking down the street, though, she had to admit, actually, no, she wasn't fine at all. In fact, she had never felt so *desolate*. "And that's bad," she said out loud. "Because I have felt pretty desolate before."

Without thinking about it, her feet found their way to the practice courts where she had watched Jakarta and Pharo so many times. No one would know where she was. So what? she thought defiantly. No one ever thought about *her* feelings. They wouldn't care if she froze to death.

She sat on a bench for a long time, shivering. "You're just feeling sorry for yourself," she whispered. It was true. But so what? If there was no one else to feel sorry for her, she'd feel it for herself.

She was surprised—and also not surprised—to hear footsteps. She was surprised—and not surprised—that it was Jakarta who cared enough to find her.

"Hey," Jakarta said, settling down beside Dakar.

"How did you know I might be here?" Dakar asked.

"Mom and Dad sent me to Melanie's house. Melanie and her mom drove over to check the magic place. I thought you might be here. Pharo walked me over." Jakarta gestured with her chin and Dakar glanced back. In the dusk she could barely see Pharo leaning against a tree. He waved.

So they had all cared, Dakar thought with relief. Then she scolded herself. "You're such a baby. Why do you make them prove themselves?"

She looked at Jakarta's face, which was wet with something. Tears? Sweat? "Why did you do it?" Dakar blurted out.

It was obvious that Jakarta knew what she

meant. "I don't know why I did it," she said, slumping over. "Coach wanted that honor for me so bad. He took a chance on me, you know. He worked hard with me. Why didn't I give him what he wanted?"

"Yes," Dakar wanted to yell. "Why didn't you?"

"But I knew Sharyn would make it." Jakarta went on as if she were arguing with herself. "We practiced that exact shot a zillion times. And that basket meant a zillion times more to her than to me. Her only game points of the season, you know."

"That's not the point," Dakar wanted to say. "Why do you have to join Dad and be the patron saint of lost causes?" But maybe it was the point. She wished she didn't feel so all confused.

After a few minutes Jakarta said, "Probably my motives weren't that pure."

She put her head in her hands, and suddenly Dakar wanted to hug her. It was hard to have a pure heart.

"I might have done it," Jakarta said, "because I wanted to show Dad he was wrong. That sports isn't all about greedy grabbing and self-glory." She laughed—a low, sad laugh. "I also have to admit I just might have done it to make Coach mad.

Because sometimes he reminds me so much of Dad, and it was all mixed up in my mind with getting back at Dad."

Dakar slid her mouth down into the front of her coat. Her breath warmed her chin and neck. "Why does everything have to be so complicated?" she said in a muffled voice.

"You know how God was always doing miracles in ancient Israel, making the sun stand still and sweeping people up in flaming chariots?" Jakarta said. "Do you know why it never seems like God does those kinds of things to save people these days?"

"Huh-uh."

"You know how the Apostles' Creed says Jesus 'ascended into heaven and sitteth on the right hand of God the Father Almighty'? Would you be able to do miracles with someone sitting on your right hand?"

"That's not funny." Dakar liked the sound her voice made inside the coat. It made her sound like a little, petulant kid—and that's what she was, she thought fiercely. Just a little kid.

"Sorry." Jakarta laughed. "I thought it was when I heard it. It's a boarding school joke." Her voice suddenly got serious. "Oh. One last thing. Some little piece of me did it because I wanted Dad to be proud of me."

Dakar sighed.

"He and I are going back to Kenya," Jakarta said.

"I know," Dakar said. That was it, she thought. That was what the desolation was about. The second she saw that last basket, even though she didn't know she knew, she knew.

"Of course, I'll stay through state," Jakarta said. "I think we might win. But I miss soccer. I miss Africa. This isn't home. Pharo promised to come visit me. His mom wants to visit, too. I wish you'd come with us."

Dakar's heart was being squeezed in half. Maybe she should go. She thought about the jacaranda trees, fat, fancy flowers drooping over the fences and onto the ground. But every place was beautiful. And people could make a difference every place, too. Even if Jakarta's name wasn't going to be on the wall o' jocks forever, look how her basketball playing had made people come out from behind their television sets and come and sit together and cheer. Look at Aunt Lily and the cook making plans to plant beans. For that matter, look how the cook got brave enough to visit her sister. I made a difference, too, she thought in amazement.

Dakar unzipped the top of her jacket and let the freezing air shock her lips. Everything else felt numb.

"Last time I went off," Jakarta said, "you came to boarding school after me. You know, Mom has Aunt Lily."

It was probably true. Mom didn't need her. But there was so much she needed to learn about Mom. And about Cottonwood.

"I'll miss you," Jakarta added. "It'll be harder when we don't have each other."

Dakar nodded. They wouldn't have each other, and they'd still have the arrows that flew by day and the pestilence that stalked in darkness and, underneath it all, the Allalonestone. "I wish you'd stay," she whispered.

"I guess we'll have to be water babies," Jakarta said softly. "Find boats and hang on."

"Jakarta," Dakar said, "do you know where the water babies go?" Her teeth were chattering, but she told Jakarta everything. About the pool. Jakarta knew that part. About how the current pulled the boats out of the pool. About the waterfall. "It's no good being water babies," she said. "Once you go over the waterfall, there's no way back home."

Jakarta sighed. Then she stood up and pulled Dakar to her feet. "You're cold."

"Freezing."

"Let's go. Pharo is probably freezing, too."

Dakar took a step. It felt strange to step on a numb foot.

"Just a second," Jakarta said, hanging on to Dakar's hand. "I remembered something. When the water babies fall into the water, they're all right. They can always go to Mother Carey. Mother Carey sits in her pool and makes old beasts into new ones."

Oh! That was what was so important about Mother Carey. The three brave things she and Jakarta had done that day in Maji were, first, to make princesses from the petunias in the enchanted, forbidden garden and, second, to go by themselves on the path to the waterfall and gather water babies. The third thing was to take everything—the princesses, the water babies, and their paper dolls—to the rain barrel they weren't allowed near because Dad said it was dangerous.

"Just this once we can," Jakarta had said. "Because it's Mother Carey's peace pool, and we need to tell Mother Carey that we trust her and we need her help."

They had solemnly put the princesses and water babies and paper dolls in the rain barrel, one at a time, saying the incantation. When they looked up, there was Mom, watching them, holding out her arms.

Dakar could feel the strength in Jakarta's hand, even though they both were wearing mittens. No matter where they decided to live, she and Jakarta would always be the red rose and the briar.

"Promise me that you'll do one thing before you leave, okay?" she said. "Promise that just once you'll come in my room and sing 'Barbry Allen.' "

TWENTY-TWO

"Tut, tut," Pharo said, tapping her lightly on the head. "Didn't I warn you about winter? Don't be scaring us like that."

On the way home Jakarta and Pharo walked on each side of Dakar and took her hands. Dakar tried to fight them off, but they wouldn't let her. Pharo held one hand, and Jakarta held the other. They swung her arms, laughing.

"Got to warm you up," Pharo said.

Dakar scowled. "Better warm Jakarta up. She's the one everyone is going to be mad at."

"They'll be mad for a couple of hours because she wasn't what they wanted her to be," Pharo said. "By tomorrow they'll be over it, hey."

Dakar stared up at the moon. It was astonishing that the whole world could turn white, like the inside of sugarcane. Everywhere she looked were different shades of white: ivory and parchment, oatmeal and bamboo. Beyond this world were the hearts of stars and the whole hundred-million-year-old universe. She shivered.

"You okay?" Jakarta asked.

Dakar nodded. It was all hard to figure out. Between the Allalonestone and the waterfalls, life was a scary place. Lots of times you didn't know the way to Mother Carey, and you couldn't always even hang on to the people in the boat with you, no matter how much you wanted to.

But the cook and Aunt Lily were right. It wasn't all bitter and terrifying, either. Sometimes it was unbelievably beautiful. She squeezed Jakarta's and Pharo's hands with her numb fingers.

She had learned one thing in Cottonwood so far, she thought. No, two. One, you couldn't get so caught up in *safe* that you forgot to be fully alive. Two, courage and kindness and friendship and truth sent magic splinters into the universe, but you had to practice them, which meant sometimes having to go on quests and sometimes even giving up and letting go. Wait. Was that two things or three?

When they got close to the house, she saw that its windows were breathing light out into the street. Mom and Dad and Aunt Lily all were looking out the front window. Mother Carey, she thought in surprise. Of course. That was the house's name.

Mom opened the door. "Thank goodness you're all okay," she called. "Come get warm."

"Thanks," Dakar said to Jakarta and Pharo, shaking off their hands. "I can go the rest of the way by myself."

Her feet were numb so that she could hardly feel the steps as she ran up them, but she knew Dad would have a fire going, and she couldn't wait to let Mom pull her inside.

ACKNOWLEDGMENTS

I would like to thank my parents for the Maji memories, most of which are very real and cherished, and my sisters and brother who played all the inventive games with me, including the water babies. Special thanks to my youngest sister, Jan, who gave me comfort and joy on recent trips to Ethiopia and Kenya and whose family interviews about our Maji years helped fill in some blanks. I deeply appreciate my older sister, Caroline, and her family for sharing their Kenya home and lives so warmly. I'm also grateful for schools—my own Good Shepherd School, the other three I visited in Addis Ababa in 1997, and two schools in Nairobi, Rosslyn Academy and the International School of Kenya, that made my Kenya trips possible and drew me gloriously in.

The town of Cottonwood, North Dakota, is fictitious. I am, however, grateful to my children and their friends for glimpses into adolescent life in the upper Midwest, since I went to high school in Ethiopia and, as my son David once told me, didn't really "get it" about junior high and high school life in the United States. Jonathan and Rebekah will especially see them-

selves reflected in these pages; a big thanks to both of
you. Thanks, also, to so many basketball teams in east-
ern North Dakota and western Minnesota for hours of
gleeful watching, especially to the teams my sons,
David and Jonathan, played on. And this book
couldn't have been written without my husband,
Leonard Goering, who sat beside me through so many
games and who has supported countless hours of writing and speaking.

Dr. Kevin Young used his knowledge of microbiol-
ogy to help me understand what I needed to know
about parasitology. I owe him thanks and take responsibility for any mistakes. Another thank-you goes to
Sam Keen, whose book *Learning to Fly* (Broadway
Books, 1999) made me intrigued with trapeze artistry
and taught me almost everything I know about it.

Finally, I owe a huge debt to my astute early read-
ers, who loved the story and told me the places where
they didn't love it. Special thanks to Franny Billings-
ley and Deborah Marie Wiles, who held my hand
through a dark writing night.

Bibliothèque de Beaconsfield Library
514-428-4460
08 août 2013 14:40

Usager / Patron : 23872000027743

Date de retour/Date due: 19 août 2013
The prophet of yonwood /

Date de retour/Date due: 29 août 2013
Jakarta missing /

Total : 2

HORAIRE / OPENING HOURS
Lundi / Monday
13:00 - 21:00
Mardi - vendredi / Tuesday - Friday
10:00 - 21:00
Samedi / Saturday
FERMÉ / CLOSED
Dimanche / Sunday
FERMÉ / CLOSED
beaconsfieldbiblio.ca
24 juin, 1er juillet, 2 septembre: FERMÉ
June 24, July 1, September 2: CLOSED